IF YOU DON'T KNOW
DIDDLEY
YOU DON'T KNOW SQUATT

DUANE LANCE FILER

Gotham Books

30 N Gould St.
Ste. 20820, Sheridan, WY 82801
https://gothambooksinc.com/

Phone: 1 (307) 464-7800

© 2025 *Duane Lance Filer*. All rights reserved.

No part of this book may be reproduced, stored in a retrieval system, or transmitted by any means without the written permission of the author.

Published by Gotham Books (February 18, 2025)

ISBN: 979-8-3484-9400-1 (H)
ISBN: 979-8-3484-9398-1 (P)
ISBN: 979-8-3484-9399-8 (E)

Because of the dynamic nature of the Internet, any web addresses or links contained in this book may have changed since publication and may no longer be valid.

The views expressed in this work are solely those of the author and do not necessarily reflect the views of the publisher, and the publisher hereby disclaims any responsibility for them.

A couple of hippies – Duane and 7-year-old grandson Lance Giovanni Filer ("Gio.") "PEACE TO EVERYONE IN THE WORLD!" In the words of Sly & the Family Stone we shout out – "'Thank You Falletin Me Be Mice Elf Again!"

CONTENT

Dedication 1

About the Author & Acknowledgements 2

Prologue 4

Preface 7

Chapter 1 Diddley Squatt's Next Life Chapter Begins 9

Chapter 2 Diddley Heads Out on the Chitlin Circuit Tour 15

Chapter 3 Welcome to Alabama 22

Chapter 4 Diddley's Delight (or Was it?)-First Chitlin Tour Experience 36

Chapter 5 Diddley Bonds with Mute 88

Chapter 6 Mute, Racism, and Welcome to Birmingham 98

Chapter 7 Concert Night at the Carver Theatre 119

Chapter 8 Next Stop #3 – Atlanta, Georgia 142

Chapter 9 If You Don't Know Diddley – You Don't Know Squatt 228

Dedication

This book is dedicated to everyONE and everyALL. It is time in this crazy world to acknowledge, as I've always felt in my heart, that when brought into this world – each individual being/baby born has absolutely no individual control of who their parents are; what their ancestors may have done or contributed; no control of their gender, the color of their skin/race, name, height, weight, city where they live, color of their eyes, hair color; pimpled skin, born rich or poor, health issues – we as newborns have no choice!

It doesn't take long after birth for each individual to realize, "Hey, I love some of these people called family and friends, but geez, I got to learn to deal with stuff on my own because I'm the only one in MY skin and know my true feelings about stuff."

About the Author & Acknowledgements

Duane Lance Filer has written a total of 9 books to date – this is his 10th book. Duane and his six siblings were raised in the great city of Compton, California by mom Blondell and Dad Maxcy (now both deceased) and the kids (Maxine, Duane, Kelvin, Stephanie, Anthony, Dennis, and Tracy) were told and taught to follow their dreams and achieve, and to never give up; to give back and contribute to their communities and society. Duane has been married to Dr. Janice Filer for over 40 years, and they produced daughter Arinn and son Lance (daughter-in-law Faviola and the newest addition to the family- grandson Giovanni.) Duane loves writing, painting funky art and portraits, diddling on his bass guitar, talking and teaching his grandson Lil Gio, all the while listening to Sly Stone and Miles Davis, loves the Lakers and all Los Angeles teams – and loves animals. Squirrels are welcome in his backyard in Carson!

➢ Duane's 9 books are:

Children's Books - The "LongTALE for shortTAILS" 7 short story collection comprised of:

- Fastjack Robinson (2015)
- Ms. Missy – Bishop's First Dog (2015)
- Duncan & the Chocolate Bar (2015)
- Lancie's Lessons by Letters (2020)

➢ Fiction –

- Square Squire and the Journey to DREAMSTATE (2012)
- Square Squire and the Journey to DREAMSTATE – Squared Version 2.0 for Teens and Young Adults (2015)
- The Legend of Diddley Squatt – A Novella from a Brother Fella (2017)

- ➢ Non-Fiction Journal – Plays/Essays –
    - The Baby Boomers First-Hand/First-Year Guide to Retirement….365 Days of Bliss (?????) or Diss (Not?????) – (2014)
    - Word Food for Doods (2018)

All books can be reviewed and obtained at Amazon, Xlibris, AuthorHouse, IUniverse, Barnes and Nobles, etc. Just google Duane Lance Filer and you will find all 9 of my books at various websites. Email Duane at duanelancefiler@gmail.com. All books can also be purchased through Duane's personal website at https://duanelancefiler.wixsite.com/duanelancefiler.

Thank you to my friend and illustrator for some of my prior nine books, Ajaye Herndon, for the picture of Diddley on the cover. Thanks also to my cousin Kyle Burson for his insight and ideas. Finally, thank you to my brothers Kelvin and Anthony, my friend Jake the Snake, and my son Lance- for listening to my rants and raves as I poured my heart into this book. Thanks to all my Fellas and various relatives for listening and responding to me through this once again crazy journey – much love!

I want to thank Pamela Samuels Young and Robert L. Johnson, a couple of local friends/writers, for their thoughts and ideas during this writing process. We keep in contact – and they are indeed two talented writers who I enjoy discussing my crazy ideas with, and I know will give me their honest opinions through this difficult process.

Lastly, I want to thank Pamela Sheppard, also a local publishing consultant, for her edits and thoughts – and for always encouraging me to be myself in my writing and to NEVER give up on my dreams! PEACE- AND THANK YOU ALL!

Prologue

"If You Don't Know Diddley – You Don't Know Squatt" is part two of my 2017 novella "The Legend of Diddley Squatt – A Novella from a Brother Fella." It follows Diddley Squatt as he embarks upon his first ever concert tour out of Mississippi on the famous Chitlin Circuit Tour. Following is a brief synopsis of the **first** Diddley Squatt book. Enjoy!

The time- backwoods deep south circa USA 1940-50's. Young Diddley Squatt is abandoned by father Doodley Squatt and mother Jackie Squatt soon after birth; left to be raised in Rundown City by his grandma **"Momma" Squatt** who runs the largest brothel, the Copp-A-Squatt Inn, this side of the Mississippi. Momma's brothel is not thought of as a "den of inequity," but rather as a cleanly run establishment that provided a needed service of great food (soul) and companionship for those souls traveling through the south (including folks of all color- businessmen, musicians, politicians, servicemen.) Diddley is loved and raised by the caring Copp-A-Squatt ladies, especially **Chastity, Delilah, Tiffany, and Epiphany**, and the goo-gaggle of interesting characters that inhabit the brothel. They teach him to be color blind and limitless with love for all God's creatures- humans and animals alike. His first friend in elementary school is **Pryor Richards**, a poor white bucktoothed kid who stands up for the bullied Diddley. Diddley quickly learns he possesses 3 unique gifts/powers at an early age: 1.) Young Didd is special/gifted and can identify God's "kindred souls" that allow him to speak and converse with certain animals who share Diddley's soulfulness. He meets and talks to **Percy the Possum,** a possum who lives in the backyard of the Copp-A-Squatt. Percy passes on the word to other animal friends; 2.) **Nate the Skate,** a Copp-A-Squatt regular who roller-blades as his means of transportation, gifts him with a special harmonica, passed down from slave ancestors, that allows Diddley to make himself small by blowing into the lowest hole; 3.) **Lady. M. Bugg (LadyM),** a ladybug who heard about Diddley from Percy and befriends him one day when she lands on him, and he consoles and welcomes her, rather than swatting and killing her. Later, she allows Didd and special friends, once "smalled," to fly on her back.

Other friends continue to help Diddley through his elementary and middle school/high school years – especially musicians who frequent the Copp-A-Squatt while passing through Rundown City. **Bobby (Robert) Johnson**, a famous blues guitarist who frequents the Copp-A-Squatt when in town, falls under Didd's spell and teaches him guitar chords and Diddley soon learns the power of music and how it helps him deal with life. Others, like **Otis Johnny**, teach him the hambone and helps Didd learn rhythm and backbone.

Then……….one day, a dying **Bobby Johnson** asks Didd for a special favor. Diddley of course obliges his friend, and with the help of LadyM, he uses his power of smallness to carry Bobby to Clarksdale, Mississippi to a graveyard known as the Crossroads. There, amid the monstrous hills of the darkened graveyard, Bobby is reunited with and hopes to make amends for sins granted to him 50 years ago- by the infamous **Mr. DeVile (a.k. the Devil)**. A dying Bobby expresses how he "souled his soul" to the Devil in return for fame/women/glamour- instead of working hard for success by practicing and working at his guitar craft; in essence he short-circuited to fame. As his last wish on earth, he wants Didd to know that wasn't the correct way; that nothing in life comes easy and your talents should come through hard work and practice- not through the selling of your soul. Alas, Mr. DeVile arrives and bellows with amazement and snobbery when once again meeting his long ago once "friend" Robert Johnson. They argue rigorously. Diddley then finds a here-to-fore unknown strength, and confronts the Devil head on by spewing Bible verses learned in Sunday School – AND WINS- leaving the Devil infuriated as he and the dying Robert and LadyM fly away. Bobby dies days later, but with a smile on his face.

High school. Diddley is growing into a handsome young man (of course he catches the school girls eyes- even those who once bullied him because of his strange name;) wearing his patched blue jeans and guitar gig bag slung around his neck and that ever-present tiny harmonica around his neck; he continues to grow in his senior high school year, involved in sports, science and math; starts busking on the streets of Rundown City for music experience; loses his virginity; then meets his first high school true love, the glorious **Glorendous Zoowalter** – she a dark-skinned Cameroon beauty - only to have her family move away. Heartbroken, Diddley thinks about the recent losses……Glorendous……the Copp-A-Squatt characters continue to disappear and die due to father time. Dark days, but then Diddley is consoled and brought back to happiness only after he meets and befriends someone who will ultimately become his best friend in life- who also happens to be a flying squirrel – none other than **Sly Squinter**. Sly becomes his trusted friend!

After graduating from Rundown City High, Diddley feels it is time for him to experience life outside of Rundown City and without the help of his Grandma and the special ladies- he needs to experience life on his own. Life lessons learned - and after the last party at the Copp-A-Squatt with the remaining characters - Didd is driven to the train station. The tearful ladies and Momma Squatt say their heartfelt goodbyes and wish Diddley good luck; kisses all around. Diddley, with his ever-present guitar bag slung around his back and his trusted harmonica around his neck, bids farewell for now. And oh yes, Sly is in his special pouch in the guitar bag, tucked away with plenty of nuts for the trip.

Onward. Didd and Sly head to Dreem City, where Didd lands his first gig at the Dreem City Little Kitty nightclub. Using the techniques learned from Robert Johnson and from nature, Diddley enthralls the crowd with known Robert Johnson tunes as well as originals, and he shreds that guitar and plays it unlike anything ever heard before. The reviews in the next day Dreem City newspapers are fantastic, raving about "this Diddley guy with amazing talent." The owner immediately signs him to a contract. Diddley Squatt is on his way, with best friend Sly (a squirrel) cozied right next to his side.

Is the world ready for Diddley? If you say "no" – then indeed "You Don't Know Diddley Squatt!"

Preface

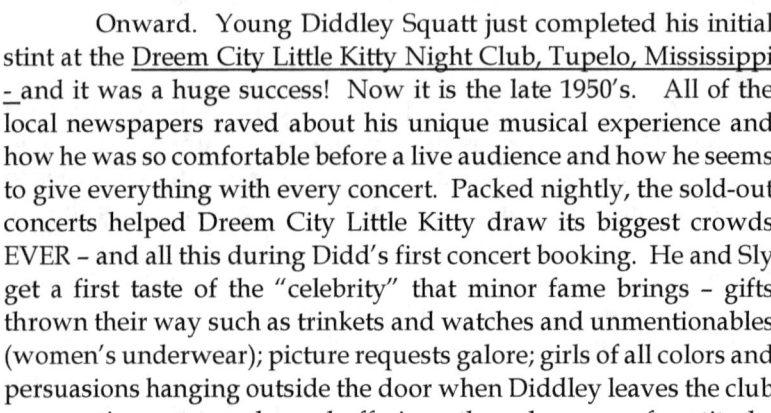

Onward. Young Diddley Squatt just completed his initial stint at the Dreem City Little Kitty Night Club, Tupelo, Mississippi - and it was a huge success! Now it is the late 1950's. All of the local newspapers raved about his unique musical experience and how he was so comfortable before a live audience and how he seems to give everything with every concert. Packed nightly, the sold-out concerts helped Dreem City Little Kitty draw its biggest crowds EVER - and all this during Didd's first concert booking. He and Sly get a first taste of the "celebrity" that minor fame brings - gifts thrown their way such as trinkets and watches and unmentionables (women's underwear); picture requests galore; girls of all colors and persuasions hanging outside the door when Diddley leaves the club - requesting autographs and offering other pleasures of gratitude. Didd takes it all in stride. Why you ask? Because of the lessons he had learned to this point. He was not about to let Momma Squatt or any of the girls at the Copp-A-Squatt down!

As a matter of fact, after every performance when he and Sly would return to his small room at night, before his head hit the pillow, he, with Sly right beside him (yes...often chewing on a nut), would drop to their knees and say a prayer - just as the girls at the Copp-A-Squatt had taught Diddley years ago:

"Dear God- although I have just started on this journey, I want to first of all give all praise and glory to you for the reason me being here. I know all things are possible only through your blessings, and I will never forget this foremost. I then must of course thank my mom Jackie and my dad Doodley – although I barely remember meeting them -but they brought me into this world, and they are my parents, so I give them glorious thanks. Then of course, I pray you look after and keep my grandma Momma Squatt safe and healthy. She is and continues to be my rock- what a great person. Also, while going through this first transformative experience in my life, I will never forget the lessons bestowed upon me by my various mentors. I must first start with the Copp-A-

Squatt ladies such as Chastity, Destiny, Tiffany the Epiphany, and of course Delilah. Lord bless these ladies. Thou some may have found their profession ungodly; they did what they had to do to survive. God loves all folks- that's why he is god! Next, no way can I lay my head to rest without mentioning all of my good human friends in Rundown City, maybe some not actual friends but who taught me valuable lessons through good and bad relationships, such as Pryor Richards, Sabrina Tuggars, Herbert Hebert, Marco Valentus, Glorendous Zoowalter, ol' Rusty Bhutt, Nate the Skate, Cecil the Beetle, and of course Robert (Bobby) Johnson.

Where would I be without my animal friends...I'm talking about Percy Possum, LadyM, and of course, last but not least, my main soul partner and kindred soul - my best squirrely friend in the world – Sir Sly. I love both my human friends and animal friends alike.

Please lord keep us all safe and on the right path – in Jesus' name...amen!

"AMEN!" chimes in Sly, "now let's hit the sheets!"

CHAPTER 1:
Diddley Squatt's Next Life Chapter Begins

Next morning after Diddley Squatt's first major performance before a live crowd. Diddley has completed the Dreem City Little Kitty tour- his first – and he has no idea what is next. He is scheduled to be out of this hotel by evening time. He and his best friend Sly, who happens to be a flying squirrel, sit on the hotel bed- bags packed – but Diddley has NO IDEA what is next? He sits there munching on the last complimentary breakfast of grits, eggs, and biscuits from the hotel – Sly on a nut of course. Sly is a very funny squirrel; and man, do they communicate through speech!

"So, what's next my human friend? We've got to be out of this joint soon," said Sly as he moves over to the arm of the sofa, squinting into Diddley's eyes.

"I really don't know. I guess I should have thought about our next move way before now. I think I've just learned a valuable lesson on how important it is to think ahead about certain things – all I was concentrating on was what the night's performance and what to play...wow, the time just flew by. What are we going to do now - where will we go? We have the money that J.J. paid me, but I should have prepared better."

"Aw.... you're a young stud....and you had nobody to guide you. You've grown over the few years I've known you. I cannot believe I made it to these years in the 1950's – nearing the 60's. We animals all take it a day at a time. Hell – I never know where my next nut will come from; I just go with the flow. However, I guess it is easier for us animals. I can live and sleep anywhere, all I have to do is climb out the window and do my business....but you humanoid beings are always thinking about what's next. And before I forget, thanks sir Didd for adding that genius squirrel potty in your gig back – genius! I've always got my fur coat on – so I don't need a warm room or covers to sleep at night. You humans have conditions that have to be met. You need money and rooms and have to buy food. Now that I'm saying this, who is the smarter breed – I'm just saying?" Sly falls over in laughter as his nut falls to the floor.

"Funny dude...you lost your nut you nut," Diddley says laughingly and throws a pillow at Sly, "and about that extra spot in my gig bag for your special needs....no problem....... Momma Squatt always taught me to clean out my stuff every morning."

Just then comes a knock at the door. Diddley moves to the door and to no one's surprise, it is the white man concert promoter J.J. Brohams.

"Diddley Squatt – my young and amazingly gifted friend, how are you" says J.J. as he rushes in, sweating and in a hurry as usual, and takes a seat in a corner chair. And of course, he is chomping on a cigar.

"I'm fine J.J., and I'm glad that you dropped by. I have some things I need to tell you sir J.J. First off, I want to give you my deepest thanks for believing in me and granting me my first gigs at your wonderful concert club, the Dreem City Little Kitty. It has been an amazing experience, and the lessons I have learned have been enriching tools I hope to carry in my tool bag the rest of my life. I have seen and witnessed so much, and because of this initial gig I hope to expand my creative abilities and keep growing as a musician and singer.

So, thank you sir. It has indeed been a blessing," said Diddley as he moved over and shook J.J.'s hand.

"See...that's why I like you. I saw this in your eyes the first time I saw you," said J.J. as he chomped on his stinky cigar, "you are a young man with manners, grace, and gratitude. I knew you had the right stuff – that's what I do! You are going to make it really big one day young man, just remember to stay on the straight and narrow. This entertainer path can be treacherous and wary. I just hope you never forget that I gave you your very first chance to reach the stars – and that if you make it big in this business, which you might, you won't forget ol' J.J. and return the favor somehow. Now I'm going to tell you something very important, so I hope you are listening," as he points his cigar at Diddley.

"You have my attention" says Didd.

"I would suggest for your next move, you need some more seasoning………and it's not good for a wanna-be performer to just sit around and practicing just his songs and craft. You need some life experiences young gun……so I suggest you hit the road and really learn about life and the struggles you will have to endure to become famous. Plus- not only are you perfecting your performance skills like singing and enhancing your guitar skills; your song writing skills – but also *learning* what the road is gonna be like and how to handle the chores of traveling and touring. You also got some life lessons to learn; and you can't do that sitting around. You gotta pay your dues like all struggling musicians…. you get what I'm saying – capeesh!" (a word J.J. often used at the end of one of his rants) he said as he extended his hand. Didd not only extended his hand- but brought J.J. in for a hug, which was something that was becoming popular among the "cool" folks.

"So now…. what I'm offering, and proposing, is to help you on this next chapter of your life. I suggest, young gun, that you hit the "Chitlin Circuit," and begin the process of performance life! No doubt you are probably asking "what in the world is the Chitlin Circuit?" Well – this new venue for black artists is probably the most revolutionary market and promotion for black artists in the world! White performers and bands have no problem when touring to promote their records – all over the country – but it isn't the same, unfortunately, for black artists. This new Chitlin Circuit is a landmark for black performers where you can perform and actually come out ahead. I'm telling you - the Chitlin Circuit is the first EVER concert tour that features black artists and where at least you can make some money.

Here's the deal – all you have to deal is agree to this simple contract I've drawn up – sign your name – and I will take care of all of the rest. You won't be disappointed young Didd," continues J.J. through his ever-present cigar smoke, "you will meet all the old blues masters, as well as the up-and-coming hep cats ready to set the music world on fire...and all you have to do is sign. I will set you up with all the concert dates; all the hotel accommodations, the food; Chitlin Circuit bus rides...everything.... just sign....and then of course – there is my FEE of 50% of everything/all profits you make at the end of the year tour. Yeah – you get paid once- at the end of the tour. This is a great deal I'm offering – anybody will tell you that. Not a bad deal at all in today's market – profitable for us both! Capeesh?!"

"Wow – that sounds great to me!" said the very excited just turned 18 year-old Didd – he had no idea if it was a good deal or not, just that it was a next step because he and Sly didn't have a "next step" or a clue what their "next steps" were.......maybe without this new deal his only move was to go back to Rundown City – after only a relatively short first time out. What else could he do?"

"Where do I sign" he offered with glee – although when he looked at Sly hidden in the corner - his animal friend had a quizzical look on his face – but of course he couldn't offer his squirrel opinion/talk in front of J.J.

J.J. pulled the contract from his suit jacket faster than you could say Fastjack Robinson! Didd signed his name and the two shook hands. Oh my!

J.J folds the newly signed contract, and before leaving says "and you can always bring your squirrel friend with you whenever you are in town. You probably thought I didn't notice him – but believe it or not- I too am a friend of all animals. However, I think you two need to have a good conversation about the do's and don'ts about traveling on the road.... other musician's may not understand your connection and may become - *"freaked out"* - as this new saying I heard some of the cats say. And, you were talking to him like you think he really understands you – yeah right – like humans and animals can actually understand each other? So, have your talk or whatever before boarding the bus later this evening at 7pm – they will swing by to pick you up and take you to your first gig on the Chitlin Line. Be out front of the hotel packed and ready – Capeesh?" he nods to Didd and heads out the door.

"Will do!" Didd says excitedly. J.J. is gone.

The door closes. Sly jumps out onto Diddley's shoulder.

"So, what was he talking about my human friend…that stuff about "others may not understand our connection" Sly says.

"I think what he brought up is an important point that we must discuss, my friend," says, Diddley. "I'm sure your aware that although we have this connection and I can hear you and you can hear me and others when we speak – folks just wouldn't believe that we can actually hear and understand each other. You do understand our unusual and surreal relationship, my friend," said Diddley.

'Of course,…but hasn't it always been this way since the very first night we met and discovered our special union that night back on the Copp-A-Squatt's back porch? What changes now?" asked Sly as he crawled directly into Diddly's face with a seriousness Diddley had rarely seen from Sly.

"I guess J.J. was just letting me – us- know- that things are going to be much busier now. Other musicians/folks on these so called "Chitlin buses" are more curious – they may totally freak out if I have as my best friend on the road- a flying squirrel with short wings more like a common squirrel.

"I tell you what," said Diddley, "Let's just lay low. You continue hiding in my suitcases/gig bag and other belongings – and I will let you know the people who may understand our relationship, if it happens at all, and when it is Ok to "come out" and be you and with what we have going on. I guess J.J. was just preparing me for how things may be different outside of Rundown City, Mississippi and other parts of the south. Sly – you are my best

friend in the world – this isn't on you – this is on me. So please....
just show yourself if/when I say it is OK to come out. Please?"
Diddley pleaded.

"I got you my backboned straight azz-humanoid," said Sly
with a wink, "and I will also continue to first find a place outside to
handle my special business cause I don't won't to give you any extra
worries – you got enough in your life – capeesh?".

"What? Capeesh? straight azz-humanoid? Where did you
hear that language before?" said Diddley with a smile on his face.

"What??? While you are up on that stage doing your thing
I'm usually up in the rafters above the crowd, running around
without a squeak. Sound rises and we squirrel have great ears.... I
can hear the brethren crowd talking. I can hear an ant fart! I'm
quite the listener. Capeesh?" said Sly laughing.

"WHAT??" Diddley and Sly both laugh - and the pillow
fight continues into the night.

Before Diddley falls asleep – he hears Sly in his ear....and
Sly whispers:

"Just one last thing – don't forget to get me some nuts for
the long bus ride!"

Goodnight."

CHAPTER 2
Diddley Heads Out on the Chitlin Circuit Tour

Diddley is packed and ready as 7pm. nears; I guess one could say as packed and ready as one might expect for an 18-year-old - we are talking about 2 suitcases that comprise ALL of Diddley's worldly possessions.... 2 suitcases full of jeans, t-shirts, underwear, PJ's and other assorted stage wear. Besides the suitcases, there is the ever-present guitar gig bag with Sly all warm and cozy in his special hidden pouch. That's it – 2 packed suitcases and a gig/guitar bag. Diddley was always expanding Sly's pouch, and it was indeed a nice hidden house for Sly whenever they traveled.

Diddley lugs his luggage downstairs into the rundown lobby of the hotel, finds a bench and sits and looks out the window, awaiting the approaching bus. Didd looks out the hotel window into the night. The stars in the sky are enormous and clear- oh what a night! He sees the starry night and can't help but feel excited for what awaits next. His mind drifts back to how he got here.........from his grandma Momma Squatt to all the girls at the Copp- A Squatt who helped raise him – Chastity, Destiny, Tiffany and Delilah....to the all the various characters and animal friends in Rundown City, Mississippi. And now? After setting house records at the Dreem City Kitty in Mississippi – he will be leaving the state for the first time in his life.

Sure enough – the bus finally arrives......comes a chugging down the main highway. To Diddley's surprise, it is not near the dream bus he had imagined. He thought it would be a nice long, extended. modern bus – tall and proud - freshly painted in bright colors with maybe "Chitlin Circuit" on both sides with names of various famous black musicians splashed on each side. Instead, the bus came roaring through, coughing smoke like an asthmatic/weather-battered/chronic/chain-smoking oldie, visiting the Copp-A Squatt Inn. The bus was an ugly green and white – badly in need of new paint – and cloaked in dirt and scrum from engine to tail – mud running from the wheels to the doors and windows. There was only one sign on the bus- at the top – it said "betty boop – betty b "– but no signs attached to either side marketing the Chitlin Circuit- at least none that Diddley initially witnessed. There was smoke coming from the crooning engine and one could easily tell this bus was one for the ages...aged...but still moving. The old crusty thing made it down the boulevard and finally stopped in front of Dreem City Kitty – wheels creaking and engine singing....it took about a minute for the engine to actually stop.

The bus door opens, and out steps this fat/disheveled/bent-over/crinkled white guy from behind the wheel. He has the whitest skin Diddley had ever seen - wrinkled; and blond hair just enough long enough to reach below the old, crusty straw-hat he was wearing on his fathead. He had on old overalls, wrinkled white and green, and in an apparent effort to try to add a bit of exquisite – a bow-tie around his uneven collar.

Jeez.

Like J.J. Brohams- the bus driver has this stinky cigar pinned to the side of his mouth like a toothpick from heaven.......smoldering. He has eyeglasses on a string around his neck; not on his head, and pushes the glasses to his face only after stopping. He has this clipboard with him and runs his eyes up and down some sort of list. He moves over to the lights under the Dreem City Kitty lights so that he can see:

"Alright.......... alright...I'm looking for a...for a what the? What kind of a dad blasted name is this....... a Diddley Squat?

"I'm Diddley Squatt right here sir," said Didd as he stepped forward and extended his hand?"

"Well I'll be" said the sideways/ brick built white man as he broke out into guffaws and huge seconds of laughter, slapping his knees, bending over repeatedly, and coughing like he might have a heart attack or stroke.

"I've heard a zillion names in my days of traveling and driving. I've driven white country singers and Baptist ministers, black gospel singers, politicians, mobsters, folks sneaking into the U.S. illegally, immigrants…doesn't matter to me what color you are as long as you pay me in green – but I've never, EVER, come across a name like Diddley Squatt. That is one *different* name young gun," said the bus driver as he wiped spit from the non-cigar side of his mouth.

"Sir…. I guess you can tell I'm used to the different reactions I get when folks first hear my name," said Diddley – not particularly upset because after 18 years he indeed had seen different reactions to his name. "I'm used to it. I'm just glad to be going on this new journey in my life."

The bus driver was obviously taken aback that Diddley didn't directly confront him.

"Well……let me say……. I'm just glad you didn't take it the wrong way," said the old white dude. "I mean no harm or disrespect – I actually like the name Diddley Squatt- it is indeed distinctive. It's just after 30 years of driving buses all over the south – you have to realize I've heard some doozies for names in my lifetime – but yours may be at the top of my doozy list. "

The bus driver then yells out loud:

"anybody else heading out on this particualr special chitlin curcuit bus? You better speak up – cause THE Betty Boop, we about to hit the road again?"

There was nobody else around….so obviously the answer was "no."

Diddley jumped aboard.

The bus driver threw Diddley's 2 suitcases into the carriage area under the bus- and I mean literally just threw them – and quickly closed the carriage space. Diddley held onto his guitar gig bag as most musicians did in those days – they were part of their livelihood and a musician never knew when a song. melody, or lyrics might come to them. Obviously Young Didley was the only pick-up in Dreem City – and the bus driver had a schedule to keep.

He jumped back on the bus behind the wheel – and started the engine. The engine wheezed and geezed as it was warming.

"Come sit right next to me – Mr. Diddley Squatt. We can get better acquainted and I can give you some tips and hints on what to expect on this next journey you are about to take. I usually don't say this to somebody I don't know, but I got a feeling about you. I can tell you're a young boy – and since you didn't take offense at my laughing about your name, I almost like you already," the old fart continued to laugh and geeez.

Didd had his gig bag slung over his shoulder (he wasn't about to leave it, with Sly, in the dusty, damp under/bus carriage) and took the open seat directly behind the bus driver. Before taking his seat, he stood and looked down the narrow alley way of the bus with seats cramped to each side….it seemed the bus went forever back. Diddley could barely make out anything, the bus was so full of cigarette smoke. He could however make-out that maybe the bus was half-full with musician cats leaning back in their seats…. some sleep………. some jugging drinks from pint whiskey bottles…. some hanging onto women with their legs spread eagle/dangling across the seats. As he struggled to look, he did indeed find some returning stares; some folks poking their heads out – probably wondering who this new young cat on the bus was. Diddley finally took the seat the bus driver had recommended and propped his gig bag in a comfortable position against the window where Sly would be cozy and could actually come out and visit with Diddley if he preferred.

"So young Diddley Squatt – my name is W.C. Valley and I'm so glad you've joined our rally. We call this old bus the "Chitlin Hilton" …. or the "BETTY B" for "Betty Boop." Anyway - are you originally from Dreem City?" said the bus driver as he tooted his horn – pushed the gas pedal to the metal (smoke scattering from the tailpipe like dust from a powerful broom battering), and the old beast began to soldier onto the highway……. "getty up betty b!" Whooped w.c.

"Glad to meet you W.C. No…I'm originally from Rundown City, Mississippi. My grandma runs the Copp-A-Squatt-Inn and that's where I grew up with help from the employees and the various customers who came to stay. I started playing guitar and Robert Johnson really helped me and gave me some valuable lessons – in life and on the guitar. He was just one of my mentors."

"You from the Copp-A-Squatt? – lordy B – I've dropped off soooo many customers there for soooo many years I can't count em. Of course, I've met Momma-Squatt – I hope she is doing fine? I've eaten my share of their fried chicken and cornbread- have mercy Ms. Percy! And Robert Johnson? You knew the great Robert Johnson? He was indeed a legend during the early days of the Chitlin Circuit- I drove for Bobby many times. Well bust my britches and poop my drawers!' said W.C. excitedly, while honking his horn along the highway.

"Robert was fantastic, and I consider myself blessed to have learned from him. Actually, this guitar sitting right in back of you was a gift from Robert. He gave it to me before he died. I will treasure it forever," said Diddley as he reached back and stroked his guitar bag.

"That's Robert's guitar? Gee willigars……you are a lucky young boy. Son-a-gun!" spat W.C. "Well- as you can see – all the musicians on this round are asleep cause we been going straight tour for the past two weeks. J.J. got in contact with my boss and I was told to stop by Dreem City to pick up this young boy – you Mr. Diddley – so that's where we are. I think you will find some friends on this Chitlin tour- but the learning doesn't come easy when dealing with musicians. Musicians are such different cats- believe me," W.C. laughs out loud as he honks his horn – "you will learn this quickly – hee haw!"

"So where exactly are we headed now?" asked Diddley.

"We are on the southeastern leg of the famous Chitlin Circuit tour my new friend.... we gonna be pushing further south and east – next stop is the crazy state of Alabama where we will be stopping in two cities – Mobile first and then Birmingham. The schedule is always subject to change, but for right now it looks like:

Mobile, Alabama – Harlem Duke Social Club

Birmingham, Alabama – Carver Theater

Atlanta, Georgia – Royal Peacock

And then onto Florida.

W.C continues: "But talking about Alabama, the best thing about Alabama to me is the food - grits, gravy, good squirrel and possum, they got some good food and diners and restaurants going on there. Of course, you will have to come in through the back door if they let you in at all – sorry about that but I just want to be truthful with you."

W.C continues: "See -as an old white man speaking to a young black kid in these late years of 1950 America - I can tell you the first thing is to be careful on who you talk to....how you look at folks....how you move around.....where you eat and where you take a leak or shit....**RULE NUMBER ONE - PLEASE DON'T LOOK AT ANY WHITE WOMEN**....just follow the advice of some of these smarter and older musicians you will meet. Having said that – career wise - the best piece of advice old W.C can give you is that once you get on stage- play your britches off and let the folks tell you whether they like it or not! The audience folks will determine whether or not you have the musicianship and talent – nobody else. Listen to how they respond, how they are reacting to what they hear and feel. These promoters and hangers-on/" girl groupies" are what I heard somebody say they now call them – don't listen to them for advice. They will tell you things just to be telling you things just to try and get closer to you and leech off any of your success. Now, the folks listening to your music, will tell you the truth!"

"Sounds like some good advice W.C. I really appreciate you talking so truthfully to me and we just met. Sounds like you've been around – and I've learned to always respect my elders and listen to what older folks tell me……especially those that have been around - that's helped me get this far," said Diddley appreciatively.

"Hot dang – thank you young stud! I know we've just met – but let's have further conversations as you move around the tour. I once had a young son who run off without listening to a thing I ever said, so I appreciate helping out any young folks." W.C. almost sounded like he was tearing up because he was so appreciative of Diddley's comments.

Diddley slumped back in his seat, figuring his talk with W.C. was good enough for an initial talk. Didd had that feeling he would get with certain people- that they were being sincere in certain talks with him. He believed W.C. was trying to help him. He knew they would have many talks over their travels- and they had gotten off on the "good foot" as the new saying was spraying.

The bus soon jumped on the highway and picked up speed. The cabin grew dark again – and since nobody was moving around in the back and Diddley had no idea how long they would be on the bus – it would be best for him to get some sleep. Before dozing off- Diddley opened the secret pouch in his gig bag to check on Sly. Sure enough, Sly was in the fetal position with his four limbs wrapped around a nut – as snug as a lug in rug. Diddley rubbed his friend's belly for good luck.

CHAPTER 3
Welcome to Alabama

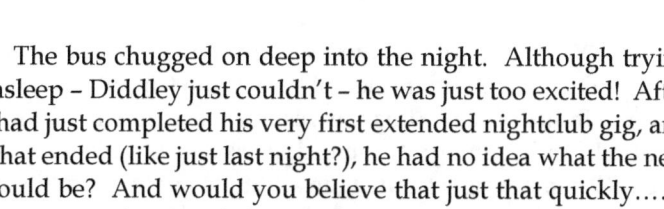

The bus chugged on deep into the night. Although trying to fall asleep – Diddley just couldn't – he was just too excited! After all, he had just completed his very first extended nightclub gig, and when that ended (like just last night?), he had no idea what the next step would be? And would you believe that just that quickly....... he was now on a bus headed to God knows where being driven by some old white cat going by the name W.C.... on the famous Chitlin Circuit? My goodness thought Diddley to himself; I may be both blessed and destined to make something of myself- but the journey isn't going to be easy......it is going to be stressful....... maybe fun......but also terrifying at the same time!

Jeeeesus.......

As the bus moved along, Diddley would occasionally hear someone in the back of the bus talking, coughing, cursing, or laughing. Sounded like not just men voices, but also some lady voices. He knew without a doubt that there were indeed women in the back of the bus; and he prayed and hoped they were singers and musicians and parts of the band – but he had no idea.

Finally.... finally...Diddly drifted off and went in to a deep needed sleep.

Sleep

Sleep

Ahhh...sleep......until:

Sometime awhile later, and it was daylight outside:

"Allright my passengers – listen up. We are in alabama, and will soon be moving into the glorious state's ditty city known as mobile, alabama."

It was definitely W. C's voice:

"We are about an hour away from the Harlem Duke Social Club – our first stop on this leg of the Chitlin Circuit. Ya'll might be hungry. Imma pull into this tiny restaurant right here before we get to Mobile and Imma grab some chicken and biscuits real quick to give ya'll something to munch on – but we got to get to the club. It will be a quick stop – but you will get something to eat"

Didd opened his eyes and sleepily looked to the left out the window. Daylight had just opened its eyes. Through glazed eyes, he seized on what appeared to be cotton fields and other, similar land he was aware? There were some cotton fields – and there were fields with horses and cows..........some mooing. The tiny restaurant W.C. just mentioned was the only building out here. He looked through the right windows- same thing – sure didn't look like any "city" land was close...actually looked like parts of where Diddley was born and raised, a.k.a. Rundown City, Mississippi. These type cotton fields were very familiar and brought back memories to the young Didd. As he gazed out, he saw black men and women- of various ages – even children, bending over and carefully extracting the cotton from the cotton plants. Didd zeroed in on the many sweating faces, many of whom looked up when they heard the whirling bus flashing by, and he felt a strange knot in his stomach. Didd's mind drifted back.....he remembered when Momma-Squatt had him pick his first piece of cotton, she warned him:

"Be careful baby and pay attention to what you are doing, watch your hands and let your eyes follow your fingers where you are placing them, because you can easily prick your fingers on the sharp thorns of the cotton plant. Now what you do is twist that round piece of cotton from the tree- it is called a boll – you twist it and yank it away and then put it in your bag. The only way to learn is to try."

Yeah, well, you can bet he punctured his fingers several times, as the blood squished down his hands! He did not like picking cotton and often felt sorry for those workers spending days in the sweaty fields.

W.C. was soon back on the bus and passed around some sacks of fried chicken biscuits ……and zoom – the Betty Boop was back on the road.

Soon………the fields started fading; and more buildings started appearing. As they continued to chug along, the fields gave way to more and more city-type/larger buildings. Diddley could tell from the smoother sound of the non-graveling tires below they were heading into more sophisticated areas. More buildings- less fields.

The bus was now moving at a slower pace, and the sounds differed…. now you didn't hear a "moo-moo" from a field, but rather a "honk-honk" of cars and taxis and screams of "get out of the way- willya" – those special city sounds of cars honking and lights blinking and people yacking and the sounds of a life of a city population. Without question, they were moving into a city area.

W.C. then spoke into a microphone he pulled from the top of the area above his seat:

"OK folks…. we should be pulling into the Famous Harlem Duke Social Club Nightclub of Mobile soon. Welcome to the great state of Alabama for any of you newcomers, and while I know most of you are oldcomers and have been here before, we definitely have at least one newcomer – because I just met him at our last stop at Dreem City Kitty (laughs and sneezes) - while most of you were asleep.   His name is (laughs)…. get ready for these folks……………… his name is…. (laughs):

" Diddley Squatt"

(laughs)……. but please be nice to Mr. Diddley Squatt

(laughs.)"

Laughter is heard throughout the back of the bus. And then the voices open up and the chatter begins from the back:

"Did W.C. say he picked up somebody named Diddley Squatt?" (man's voice – laughter.)

"Yeah...I think that's what he said...Diddley Squatt" (woman's voice - laughter)

"Really??? Diddley Squatt ??" (both men and women voices.)

"I've heard some strange names during my days, but never a Diddley Squatt" (voice- laughter.)

"Nothing surprises me on this Chitlin tour" (female voice- laughter.)

"OK....... enough of the fun folks....... relax.... we should be pulling into the civilized city of Mobile in about an hour. Thanks for your patience." said W.C.

Diddley is, of course, sitting right in the front of the bus - and doesn't flinch or turn around. He has been through these instances his whole life- and it really doesn't faze him much. Why should older voices bother him after all the younger bullied voices he's heard?

"Stay strong my kindred soul," Diddley hears Sly's familiar voice coming from a bag amongst the laughter and frolicking.

"Of course, that's my role," Diddley says while eliciting a giggle himself. "Hey wait a minute........'kindred soul – that's my role' – hey wait - that would sound good in a song. Where's my journal; let me jot that down (Didd grabs his ever-present journal and scribbles.) Anyway, as you know, all this talk does is give me strength and courage to go onward and I'm sure once I meet some of the performers and show them I belong, they will one day dread their laughter."

"You are one strange cat Diddley!" says Sly," from the bag as he jumps on Didd's shoulder, "and you certainly have more restraint and self-control that any other animal I've ever met. If my possum, or raccoon.... dog.... cats...bird...horse friends......if they were ever made fun of the way these humans treat you in front of me...... there would be duels to the death! Horses kicking.... possums/cats/dogs licking and biting.... I'm talking about some serious fights. All the years I've been with you – never seen you raise your voice, let alone a fist? Sigh......very strange cat Diddley – very strange dude. Let's catch this last hour and sleep before we hit Mobile - rest my friend!" Diddley feels Sly pat him on the back......they both laugh. Sly jumps back into his gig bag.

They doze off for the last ½ hour before hitting the real city of Mobile, Alabama!

The bus finally starts to slow as the bus tires adjust from the long country gravel "bump-a-hump" to a more street savvy "slick-a-brick" – obviously the bus is now traveling on the smooth city streets of Mobile.

Over the bus's speaker comes W. C's voice once again:

"OK, you city slicking, chain-smoking, moonshine drinking, lady-hugging bugging musicians- we'se pulling into the parking lot of the world-famous Harlem Duke Social Club. The trip took longer than expected, and since many of yawl are expected to hit the stage in a matter of hours, we thought it best to come to the Club first – and then we will head to the motel after many of yawl perform. So, wake up – put those drinks down – snuff those cigarettes or whatever it is you are smoking, out- and let's get ready to jam....... hee- haw!"

Since Diddley was in the front, he was the first one to get off the bus, even before W.C. He stepped down off the bus, after slinging his gig bag over his shoulder, and looked up high and the sign above read:

"Welcome to the world-famous Harlem Duke Social Club"

Didd was impressed while looking to the top of the old looking auditorium. The building was painted a rusty black and brown – neat, but badly in need of a paint job. Underneath the welcoming words on the marque were the words:

"Tonight, the world-famous Harlem Duke Club is proud to present the southern leg tour of the chitlin circuit. Come see some of your favorite bands and musicians – such as king d.d., stan the lizard man, dorethe a doolidge, comedian slappy fox, jack leg batey, sam bluester, and of course the treach and Tessa treu revue - and a host of other musicians."

"Wow," said Diddley, as he continued to stare at the marque and hope that one day his name Diddley Squatt would one day make the marque. Just then, Sly stuck his head out of the gig-bag……and he looked up at the marque …. squinted his squirrel eyes….and his first words since whenever were:

"Who the hell is King D.D. and Sam Bluester? These guys are stars? And they laugh at your name with names like that? And your name isn't close to being mentioned on the marquee? Hell - guess you belong in the "host of other musician's" Didd?" said Sly as he laughed slyly, "but more importantly, can you please find me some fresh nuts or just let me out of this goddamn bag and this bus and I'll explore this Mobile, Alabama city myself and get me some fresh food. We squirrels know how to take care of ourselves!'

"Rest easy Sly…we are moving into the club…I'll let you out soon and you will be free," said Diddley, "now get your head back into the bag until we figure out who may or may not be friendly with me traveling with a squirrel. Let me feel out some of these folks on the bus."

Next off the Chitlin Hilton came W.C. He offered these words to Diddley: "Just stand to the side young Diddley and watch as the folks depart – you might learn something just from watching them depart."

Didd stood to the side of the bus while those in the back started to depart. He was excited to finally see the faces of those who had hunkered in the back all these hours; many of whom had laughed at his name – but he was just glad to finally see some fresh faces.

First-off the Chitlin Hilton:

This gangly looking, red haired, young white dude dressed in blue overalls, a dirty t-shirt, no coat – wearing boots with gloves at the ready. He had curly bangs hanging over his forehead, and the greenest eyes Didd had ever seen on a human being. He smiled a nice warming smile at Didd when they first made eye contact, and one could immediately notice the red freckles all over his face. He didn't say a word as he exited the bus, but he did wink at Diddley and they smiled at each other.

"That's the stage guy who handles breaking down and moving all the equipment off the bus, then onto the stage, and setting up all the stuff; and then removing the equipment after our last performances and loading it back onto the bus for our next stop. He's been on the road with us for some time.... the new name they are calling his job is "roadie" – and he's a real roadie for sure, if I say so myself," said W.C. as he took a long puff off his cigar, turned his head, and spit into the gutter long and strong.

"He's been with us forever, and he's a fantastic worker- He can even play a little bit of every instrument and helps tune up a lot of the musicians instruments before they hit the stage.... he can play a little. Only thing though- he doesn't speak. Can't say a damn thing. We call him Mute. The story is that his daddy was a bad, bad man.... didn't like anybody talking back to him and liked to drink, and one day when his momma was being slapped around by this bad man daddy, Mute, the oldest child and only eleven- years old, had enough and stepped in and told his daddy " We've had it with you....don't hit our momma anymore!" Well, Mute's daddy got a knife out the drawer and cut off ½ of Mute's tongue. The bad ass daddy was finally thrown in jail – but Mute could never fully talk again.... He can spit out some words, but mainly just murmurs and moves his hands and eyes- and you can eventually reckon what the mute is trying to tell ya."

W.C. continued:

"Mute is a great worker. And you will quickly see - although he can't really talk, he has learned to talk to everybody by using these crazy hand signals up and down his body and his face area.... he can also murmur out some gangly-goo words....... he will also mouth his words and you can follow his mouth – it's weird. I know it sounds funny, but once you meet and get to know him, you will see EXACTLY what I mean.... the guy can talk mainly with his hands, eyes, and his mouth without saying a word. These folks love Mute – cuz he is so loyal and a hard worker...you'll see. Anyway- that's Mute."

Mute once again smiled and glanced at Diddley – his instinct was he knew W.C. was describing him to the newbie Diddley.

Second person off the bus was this old black cat wearing a rumpled old suit – stingy brim hat tucked sideways on his old grey head, with his left hand carrying a satchel of clothes slung over one shoulder, and his right hand a bottle of whiskey - half-gone.

"Hi sir," said Diddley, before W.C could even introduce them, "do you need any help. My name is Diddley Squatt – glad to meet you."

"Oh, so you are Diddley?" said the old cat with a gentle laugh," naw young blood- I can make it – but thanks for offering. I been handling my own for almost forever, however, that says a lot about you offering thou. My name is King D.D., and I play the blues; the best blues you obviously never heard," he said as he chuckled, coughed, and spat out a wad of spit larger than anything W.C. had spit prior or Didd had ever experienced. That spit flew into the gutter, bounced off the concrete, and flew five feet it was so strong and long. Like W. C's earlier spitting saga, I guess this spitting thing into the gutter thing was a regular habit in Mobile.

"That one was long overdue," said King D.D., "that was a long ass bus ride. Shit…I'll talk to you later – let me get my old ass in this club and get ready. Diddley Squatt – we will talk later," said King D.D. as he, and his whiskey bottle, and slung bag of clothes, entered the door of the club.

Third and fourth persons off the bus- one was like someone Diddley had never seen before? Remember now, Diddley had seen and met all types of different characters who dropped by during his 18 years growing up at the Copp-A-Squatt-Inn in Rundown, Mississippi - musicians, politicians, athletes, military folks…you name it – but this dude who just stepped off the bus with this latest gal – WOW! First off- the young lady clad in a short dress, short blouse, short hair, but beautiful long legs- stepped off before the man to make sure he wouldn't tumble. She held his hand and guided him down as he stepped off the bus. The lady didn't say a word.

This black negro dude looked like he was 40-years old or older. His face was perfectly shaved, with a perfectly trimmed black mustache over his crispy brown lips, sunglasses over his eyes so Didd couldn't really see his eyes. He wore a brown-satin covered stingy-brim hat cocked to the side, with a feather stretching out from the side – sharp as sharp could be! Thus, dude had on a brown, sparkling satin suit, with sparkles all a glitter over his pants and jacket; a starched white shirt – open at the collar (no tie) ……had rings on every finger…. earrings in both earlobes, brown-and white patent leather shoes – one shoelace white, the other shoelace brown. He had a cane that he used to help gauge the ground as he stepped down….and the young woman helped guide the cane to the ground.

As this character finally reached the ground, he turned and looked directly at Diddley – although Diddley couldn't see his eyes through the brown stained-tinted eyeglasses. He spoke to Diddley before moving to the club door.

"So.... Maybe we will talk in the future- maybe not – but I imagine you are the Diddley Squatt- right? From all the chatter on the damn bus you gotta be Mr. Squatt. Let me tell you this first-off – while I wish you luck in your musical endeavors, I hope you realize that the only reason you are here, it's because of musicians like me....the great Treach and Tessa Treu Revue, who helped grow this Chitlin Circuit tour, and I hope you show the proper allegiance to me and others musicians you will meet in time, and to give us our proper respect. You wouldn't even be on this bus but for our greatness – so always show respect. Listen to others around you, and maybe one day you can make something of yourself. However, my very first piece of advice to you, would be to think about changing your name. With a name like Diddley Squatt, you can't possibly think about a future musical career. When I sit on the toilet and shit, I often let out a "holy didley squat" once I'm finished. You can't be serious with that name......I'm just saying. So....... let's talk in the future – but I hope you enjoy the set tonight by Sir Treach and the Tessa Treu Revue. We like to blow people's MINDS!!!!"

Treach Treu then let out a guttural laugh:

"baaaauuuuggghhhhh" - that rattled the city walls!

Treach then stepped into the club like a royal majestic duke.
Next off the bus trampled a goo-gaggle of women; some beautiful, others rather rough looking; but as they exited, they ALL happened to spy Diddley looking inquisitively and most gave him various looks – some odd, some nods – some even blew kisses.

Here's what Young Didd saw of the women:

some were in sandals, some in heels,

some carrying clothes, others carrying bills $$$,

some were short, some were long,

some were silent, others sang a song,

some were young, others a faint old,

some with their skin-tight, some with extra folds,

some of them laughed, while others were obviously drunk,

some smelled perfume beautiful, while a few of them stunk

A very few were white, a few more were brown

but most were black, like from Didd's side of town

They all gave him a wink as they stepped down

I guess it was the usual ritual when you meet a new brown

Like my Grandma Momma Squatt told me – you reap what you sow,

I was raised to respect and to love all

So- it was if they knew – I would be there to help should someone fall,

I can't be but what I was taught, and how I was raised,

And that was to love, not pre-judge, and give God all my praise!

The girls winked and sashayed as they stepped off the bus and got a glimpse of Diddley.... some even commented:

Lady # 1: "So, this is Diddley Squatt? My goodness, you were all the talk when W.C. first introduced you over the funky sounding speaker- I must admit I did laugh when I heard your name, but wow, you are one handsome young man. Can't wait to get to know you better Mr. Squatt" – as she swept her finger across his cheek.

Lady # 2: "Diddley Squatt? Wow...you don't look like I imagined. I've got some twatt you might want to one day swat" – then a kiss on the cheek.

Lady # 3: "Hello Mr. Squatt. I can't wait to get to know you better. With a name like Diddley Squatt, I'm sure you have all kinds of stories. My first piece of advice to you – and I hope you remember this – is to start writing down some of your experiences and use them in your music- any songs you may want to write. There is nothing in this music business that makes better songs than real-life experiences, and that's the truth! The blues was born on songs from every-day black folks experiences and what they went through. We can talk later.... but just remember my words on this, our initial first meeting today!"

Now this Lady #3 really stuck in Didd's head! She was the first lady off before Treach. While beautiful, she gave him some sound advice instead of just talking about name or looks. And Didd noticed she used proper language and grammar, and seemed really sincere in her words. This lady really, really, really stuck in Didd's mind! Why? Because Lady #3 was indeed unlike all - she was exotic looking; she had piercing brown eyes, and while Ladies # 1 and # 2 and all the prior ladies who stepped off the bus or most of the black ladies in the business Didd had met in his prior life- Lady # 3, unlike all the previous, HAD SHORT HAIR and wore no make-up? She chose to showcase her beautiful, natural brown cheekbones and African -nurtured features......no long, fake wigs did this woman wear! Her short hair was cut at the side and back, slick and yet fluffy, and she let some curls run just over her left eye. From her ears dangled these beautiful long earrings. Since she didn't have a wig to distract, one could see the beauty in her *face and naturalness*. No make-up, just pursed beautiful lips, sparkling white teeth, and a smile that could melt any young man (or older man's) heart. Just plain natural beauty uninhibited and showcased – here she was as God had made her.

And her dress? No short skirt with stockings stuffed underneath.... she wore just a plain skirt that punctuated her beautifully curved hips, legs, and thighs. On her feet? No stumbling, incredibly high-heeled shoes to stumble through the day – but rather some sensible sandals that punctuated her tanned calves and manicured feet. Her blouse? No stingy, short bouncy blouse, cut at the top to expose her breasts - but rather a colorful, brightly colored African type garb (I later learned was called a "dashiki") covered her top. It all accented her hair....... her face......her earrings......her skirt....... her legs.....her feet. While others may not have seen or felt the contoured matchings of her skin-tone and outer wear – young Diddley surely noticed!

Lady # 3's last words to Diddley on this day were surely inspirational:

"So, we can talk later – but today is an important day for you as you play your first set before these new Chitlin Circuit professionals who will be hearing you for the first time. So just show them your best – and I'm not trying to put any excess pressure on you – but today's gig is a BIG deal in your life. Play from your heart and show these folks on the bus what you are about, and that you are here for a reason. My name is Tessa Treu, and I sing with the Treach & Tessa Treu Revue, and I'm sure you will do great. The girls you saw earlier are our back-up singers. The very rude guy you met earlier is unfortunately my husband – the leader of our band which we need to support our families – Treach Treu – and just believe me – ain't nothing "true" about that man whatsoever! He is my husband. He gets drunk on these bus rides – but it is out of all of our hands. The women love him and we get the bills paid. Que sera sera," said this golden lady as she swept by Diddley and gave him a quick kiss on his cheek. It was a *loving* person's kiss - not a sexual kiss......a kiss Diddley will never forget.

The processions continued - other musicians and other girls, guys.... just a bunch of all types of others......struggled off the bus. Diddley was sure he would meet all these other performers later and learn their names – but for now – it was just get off the bus!

Wow. Diddley gathered his equipment...his stuff....and moved in line behind the last folks. It was time to prepare for his first playing gig on the Chitlin Tour, at the Harlem Duke Social Club!

CHAPTER 4
Diddley's Delight (Or Was It?) : First Chitlin Tour Performance Experience

Diddley finally arrived at his "dressing room" at the Harlem Duke Social Club. The Harlem Duke was not a large venue- it was a medium sized neat/tidy club. While the other performers may have had an actual dressing room, composed of maybe a room with an adjoining area for guests or a bathroom – Diddley's room was slightly bigger than a closet at the Copp-A-Squatt Inn where he was raised. As a matter of fact, it appeared to actually be an old closet because as you entered the door, the room wasn't but about 15 feet long. Diddley opened a cabinet door at the far end of the tiny room and indeed he saw some old buckets and mops – definitely an old bucket closet.

Sly jumped out of his pouch once the door was closed and secure and of course he gave his opinion:

"GOOD GOD! I thought we were moving on up, but I guess that is reserved to the privileged and more experienced of those on the tour?

"Reserved and privileged? There you go again - when did you learn to speak in a much more higher-up tone" said Diddley as he burst out laughing while putting his gig bag and small suitcase in the corner, and hung up his one good jacket and pants on hangers on a bar to the right.

"Remember...all I can do is listen – I can't speak my mind," said Sly as he scampered around the tiny dressing room and surveyed the limited area which would be their home for the rest of the night. "You know squirrels have big ears - so I try to use them to my advantage. When all the folks are talking all over all these buses and stuff we are on – I try to pinpoint something new and interesting somebody is saying. I don't need to hear anymore stories about "this chick stood me up" or "this dude owed me $50 and I wasn't going to wait any longer" .... that stuff is boring. So......when we stopped at that restaurant before coming to this joint, you may have noticed the couple sitting outside on the bench. The lone black couple? It was an older black couple, and the woman mentioned that she was so proud of her husband who had just retired as a teacher from some black college called Tuskegee? Didd.... did you know they have black colleges in the south?

"I had heard somebody mention that one day at the Copp-A-Squatt – but I had never checked into it further?" said a surprised Didd.

"Yeah...apparently it is true," said Sly as he reached into his pouch and pulled out some cut up fruit Didd had prepared. "This Tuskegee is known as an 'historical black college'" and young black kids like yourself can go and get a college degree and hopefully find better jobs. So, while this black retiring college professor guy was talking, he mentioned the words reserved and privileged – so now these words are part of my squirrel's vocabulary. I like to expand and find new words and to learn about stuff – it's a squirrel's world my human compadre," said Sly as he jumped on the counter and winked at Sly.

"You never fail to amaze me my best friend Sly.... where would I be in this world without you?" said Diddley as he held out his hand, "give me some skin my kin," as Sly held out his open paw and slid it against Didd's open palm.

"This is definitely an old broom closet my bestie, probably reserved for the rookie and newbie on the tour."

"Bestie and newbie? I assume these are new words again" said Diddley.

"Yeah – but I didn't hear these from the retiring professor or his wife at the restaurant. I heard these from those folks on the bus talking on the long ride we just finished. While you may not have been the main talk on the bus- however, your "Diddley Squatt" name definitely had folks wondering. I think that's a good thing."

"Good thing?" So, you think it was a good thing of them laughing at my name and wondering who this strange young kid was sitting in the front of the bus and what was he doing traveling with these well-known musicians on their way to a stop on the famous Chitlin Tour? How is that a good thing?" said Diddley as he moved to the lone mirror in the cramped closet and looked at himself.

"It is a GOOD thing!' said Sly, "I heard people discussing that any type of talk, either positive or negative, about a person's name - I think they called it "publicity" - is good for a new performer trying to break into the business. Positive or negative – doesn't matter - as long as the name is mentioned. I want to tell you now- and please listen – your weird ass name of DIDDLEY SQUATT will help you in the long run. Other wanna-be performers change their names in hopes of gaining fame. You? Hell – you were born with the name Diddley Squatt. Use your weirdness as an advantage - which I think you have already been doing in your life, even if you never realized it. Different can be good.... just remember that...you think I wasn't teased like you wouldn't believe when I was little when my mom and father - my father whom like you, I never knew.... ahem.......named me Sly? What kind of name is Sly, especially for a squirrel? I just hope maybe one day somebody will remember my name and not be ashamed.... you know I like family and, and I never told you, but my last name was "Pebbles" ....maybe something like "Sly and the Family Pebbles"...I dunno" said Sly as he did a couple of back-flips.

"Alright my bestie, let's calm down; this room is not that bad. We won't be staying here long anyway, we need to get to the stage and check out the acts we will be touring with for awhile. Man.......I can't WAIT to see and hear some new music and see the acts during their performances. You know you learn by watching – that's what Robert Johnson and all the folks at the Copp-A-Squatt always told me.... learn by watching and listening. So let's get to the ballroom and take a listen to the first act.......I think it is King

D.D." Diddley pulls his good jacket off the rack/bar and exhorts Sly to come over. "So, come my 'Bestie' to your inner pouch home and let's hit the stage," said Diddley as Sly bounds over and jumps into the open pouch inside Diddley's inner jacket – the pouch the ladies at the Copp-A-Squatt had sewn specifically for these purposes.

HARLEM DUKE SOCIAL CLUB

They enter through the backstage area of the world-famous Harlem Duke Social Club. Wow. Diddley had not seen such a majestic hall in his life – although again it wasn't an overly large club- compact – yet easily the biggest "club" Diddley had ever been. The ceiling was higher up. The ceiling was white with those new "popcorn" white bubbles that were becoming popular. The bar was in the back from the stage. There was actually a small dance floor right in front after the stage… Behind the dance floor were indeed individual tables seating 4 or more. Then there were individual seats behind the tabled seating for the cheaper seats; those who just needed a peek at the musicians and any other dancer, but mainly to just enjoy the live music. What was weird" - there was even a small balcony up top for any overflow? It was a rectangular room with spotlights speared down on the stage…. this was no joke! Without question, although not big, it was to Diddley the largest venue Diddley had ever been in and the largest he would perform in to date.

In no time at all the venue was filling with those coming to hear the music of the day. They came from all over; from the train station just down the street………some on buses……some on rails…….and of course, some of the wealthier patrons who drove up in slickly painted, spit shined orange and black Cadillacs; Red Seville, Orange and Black Corvettes. And, to Diddley's delight, some of the younger folks wore "jeans" which were just becoming a hit in the States. These youngsters, some paper coined the phrase "hipster types", were talking jive and street language and slapping 5's pulling out bottles of legal alcohol and are just having a really good time – in expectation of the night to come.

Diddley, with his gig bag slung over his shoulder snug in a bug (he was carrying it because he wanted to make sure Sly was present for this important night. (Sly was indeed in his pouch – where he could look out and see- but nobody could see him.) had a great spot to the left of the stage where he could see the performers as well as the audience. Robert Johnson had taught Diddley that it was important to see how the audience reacts when certain performers were on stage- and to look into the audience's eyes and judge how they were reacting to the songs and antics on stage. If the guitarist dipped and moved and the women started to swoon – then Diddley should copy that move and use it during his performance.

"It's Ok to copy and steal from the best – it's always been done and will continue to be done" Bobby J had mentored Diddley, "then one day, when somebody steals from you – you will know you have made it – and don't get mad at them."

Diddley and Sly are firmly positioned and ready for the show to begin. They actually have some of the best seats in the house- backstage right -out of the way – where other performers were traditionally always allowed to sit and watch their fellow performers. When the Harlem Duke Social was full to the brim – A BELL RANG AND OBVIOUSLY the audience knew what this meant. Folks started clapping and the lights dimmed....... just a couple of lights over the stage and a black curtain. Then, to Diddley's surprise, a very small figure walked to the center of the stage and grabbed a microphone. Diddley's first thought was this was a black patron's child who had got loose- but then Didd noticed that the figure was dressed in a full tuxedo and when he turned from side to side, it was indeed a man... a little man of sorts. Diddley heard someone call out "he's a midget" and people laughed- but Diddley didn't laugh. DIDDLEY DIDN'T LIKE FOR PEOPLE TO CALL OTHER PEOPLE NAMES – AND HE JUST KNEW the word "midget" as not a good word. The little guy didn't seem to be bothered at all.......like Diddley being bullied because of his name, he assumed the little man had heard it all before also. His dress was immaculate and the little guy had a properly trimmed mustache and a bowtie that stood out. He just grabbed the microphone and continued in a high pitched, squeaky voice:

"Ladies and Gentlemen, the world-famous Harlem Duke Social Club is proud to host this first southern stop of the world famous Chitlin Circuit Tour. My name is Petey Pete, but many of you know me as Pee-Wee. We want you to enjoy yourselves this evening, and clap and dance – do what makes you happy – as long as you remain respectful and peaceful. The Harlem Duke is a graceful place that showcases the best in black music, and we will always continue to showcase the stars of the day. Are you ready to have a good time?"

"YEAH" yelled the crowd in unison.

"THAT'S WHAT I LIKE TO HEAR!" said Little Pee-Wee. So tonight, we have for you 8 of the Chitlin's Circuits most exciting acts. Some will perform longer than others – but believe me ladies and gentlemen – you will get your money's worth tonight. You will see in order none other than:

Blues singer and great guitarist – none other than King D.D.

The great black magician Stan the Lizard Man

Treach and Tessa Treu Revue

Doreathea Doolidge- Opera Singer

Slappy Fox – Comedian

Jack-Leg Batey- Dancer

Sam Bluester – Blues singer

Diddley Squatt

"So – let's get started with our first performers. Let's welcome to the stage – one of the world's greatest blues guitarist and singers - none other than the great King D.D. and the Mississippi Blues Hounds."

King D.D.

The curtains were pulled and there in their full glory were the Mississippi Blue Hounds – the band for all the acts, featuring a drummer, a pianist, an upright bassist, a cat who played both trumpet and saxaphone, and an older black lady back-up singer dressed in all-black top and skirt. King D'D. then strode on stage with his guitar slung over his shoulder. He was dressed in all purple tonight- purple shirt, tie, jacket, and pants- except for his shoes- black and white patent-leather shoes shined to a tee! The place erupted with applause as King D.D. strutted to the microphone.

"I'm King D.D. and these are the Mississippi Blues Hounds. We came to Mobile, Alabama to share some of our Mississippi blues with you Alabama folks. The blues is pretty much the blues no matter what state you are from, am I right about it!

"YEAH" came the raucous response.

"So, let's get started with one of my most famous songs – "My Blues is Your Blues." One……two…. three…four," as King D.D. let loose some guitar blues chops and the gig was on. D.D. sang:

"My blues is your blues

Baby, is that really any new news?

So, please let's stay together and work it out

No need for us to jump, fight, cause a scene – and shout!

Cause we all have one blues or another

Be it with a mother, father, wife, son, or a brother

But the blues is as common as a snake or a river

Doesn't' matter if you are a taker or a giver

Just remember my blues is your blues

And it might be red, blue, brown, yellow- even green

Maybe purple, black, orange- maybe a color never seen

But my blues is your blues

I don't give a rat's ass if you black, yellow, brown or white

The blues is gonna bite you sooner or later- and you all know I'm right!

So just remember that my blues is your blues

And let's all join together and sing while we battle

Cause if your blues is my blues

We ain't no babies in the fight- time to put down those baby rattles!

And only the blues can make you dream

So put aside your troubles, cuz we ALL on the same team"

The crowd explodes into applause at just these few lyrics, and the foxy ladies in the audience are sashaying to the right and left – lifting their dresses and showing a little bit of what's underneath, and their men friends are searching for places to touch.

Diddley is left muttering to himself "how in the world can one simple song……and only two verses of the song…. get the crowd so aroused so quickly?"

King D.D. eyes Diddley to the side of the stage and winks at him at that exact moment, as if to say "see…. you playing with the big boys now Diddley Squatt. You gotta bring the real deal to the table. This ain't no Rundown City shit…these folks know the real deal!"

King D.D, plays on for another 30 minutes and Diddley must admit this wild man can control an audience – just by hitting a particular note on his guitar, or by talking and conversing with the crowd in-between songs. King D.D. continues:

"I know Alabama ain't the safest town for us Negro folk, but tonight I want you to just throw away your fears and have a good time. Shake off that Jim Crow shit and crow and dance like the funky chicken we all raised! Hell…tonight is let loose time – ain't nobody gonna bother you when you in this hall. You foxy gals shake them hips – and purse them lips- do your little nips- and just let it all rip! All my brothers out there – wave your hands and finger pop all them special places – down from the hips to your shoe laces – cuz we here to touch all yall's bases – all we ask in return is a smile on everybody's faces!"

"Yeah…. this King D.D. cat can really rap!" Diddley heard Sly murmur from his pouch. "He is talking some straight talk and the people are eating it up."

"I agree my good friend," said Diddley, "but the main thing is he can also play and sing and command the stage. So, I am definitely taking some mental notes....to be a good entertainer you must have various skills of talent, but also be a people person. I will have to open up more."

"That's what I've been trying to tell you!" said Sly excitedly..., "entertaining is an art. You got it all in you Diddley – just open up your heart and let it all out."

"I'm learning," said Diddley" but I'm just naturally shy and quiet. But you are right.... if I want to grow as an artist, I must open up myself and be true to my feelings. We will see."

King D.D. finished his set and got a standing ovation. He left the stage sweating as he slung his guitar around his back. The curtain closed behind him. As he passed Diddley to the side of stage heading to his dressing room, he actually offered up some encouraging words.

"Now – that's the way you do it youngblood. You leave it all on the stage – FOR EVERY PERFORMANCE. These people don't have a lot of money, and when they buy their ticket, be sure to give them all you got. We as black folks don't need to be short-changing anybody.... we been shortchanged all of our lives. Be blessed to be out here on this stage, and not out in that sweltering field picking cotton we passed getting here or in that steaming factory doing factory work. You owe it to yourself and your folk!" said King D.D. as he staggered to his dressing room exhausted.

"I thought he was gonna be an asshole....... but I think he gave you some pretty good advice," said Sly as he climbed out of the pouch onto Diddley's shoulder – nobody was around – so nobody could see a squirrel perched on Diddley's shoulder.

"Wow, said Diddley," that was pretty nice of him to offer me some advice. And I *really* enjoyed and learned some stuff from his set. Like Momma-Squatt and the girls told me before we left Rundown City – don't judge anybody too early on this next journey.

I'm keeping an open mind, and King D.D. just proved it. You hear me my brother?"

"Loud and clear my humanoid...." humanoid" is another word I heard somebody on the bus mention. While you are learning your craft – I am also learning through these astute ears God gifted me with. Just a quick reminder though – we running low on nuts so sometime later tonight you gotta get me some bread crumbs or something to stock up on. Capeche?" laughed Sly.

"You nut...what would I do without you," said Diddley as he nuzzled Sly." O. K.... back in your hole my friend....the next act is about to perform."

The miniature small figure Pee-Wee and/or "MC Little" – once again took the stage:

"Next up ladies and gentlemen is the famous magician Stan the Lizard Man, who will show you some tricks and licks that will leave you with ticks and shitting bricks (laughter.) You won't believe some of this stuff. So...without further ado- take it away Stan the Lizard Man:

Stan the Lizard Man

The curtains opened and there in the middle-stood Stan the Lizard Man behind a simple 6 ft. long table in front of him. Stan was a light skinned black man, maybe in his 40's or 50's, shirtless, but luckily had on some reptile induced shorts that covered his midsection, but then when you ventured down-ward he exposed his naked legs, feet and toes. Stan did not possess the best physique- as a matter of fact – he had this huge pot-belly and hairy arms and legs. On the ground were a couple of boxes where he kept his props – but those were the only material objects on the stage with Stan. Now – let's discuss living objects? That was a different story……...because all over Stan roamed DIFFERENT SIZED LIZARDS over his shoulders, his arms, his waist, his legs…. his feet. These lizards were green and yellow; black and brown – red and orange, grey and purple. Some were large…others smaller and faster – but they just ran around Stan's body, and for some reason, they seemed tame and were happy with just running over Stan's body?

The crowd was silent……. what could they say or do?

'WOW," said Sly as he jumped on Sly's shoulder, "look at all my lizard brothers and sisters? It looks like they aren't afraid at all? How the hell does this Stan Man control them to keep them from running away or all over the stage? Can't wait until he starts saying exactly what his gig is," said Sly as he ran to Diddley's other shoulder.

Stan the Lizard Man continued:

"Ladies and gentlemen, my name is Stan and I'm the Lizard Man. No need to be afraid of all my lizard friends you see exploring my body – these are my best friends in the world. If you are wondering how I got to this point, when I was a little lad living in the dirty hills of South Carolina, I didn't have many friends growing up. We lived in a shack – and my daddy worked in some mill someplace. We had hills, mills, and beaches……so lizards were everywhere. My momma raised us and worked as a nanny in one of the homes up on the hill – but for some reason, one day when I was outside playing and it was hot…and this lizard ran right by me. Instead of being scared - I laughed like you wouldn't believe. I picked up the lizard…and then other lizards ran over. I had some extra cornmeal left-over from breakfast – and when I spread it out on the road – all these lizards came running out. I fed them, and then they started running all over my body. IT TICKLED. Lizards and I were friends from this instance to this exact day ever since. I later learned that lizards were Ok if you were OK and that you should never pick them up by their heads or their tails."

"So, let me show you 3 tricks with my lizard family," says Stan.

Stan, still with various lizards crawling all over his body, moves over to one of the cages and pulls out four green, red, yellow, and red lizards that sprint out and run to the tops of his shoulders – two on each side.

"Now these lizards are from the Gecko family – and they can actually talk and sing. Watch this:

Stan starts waving his fingers into the Gecko's eyes, trying to scare them…and it obviously works because the Gecko's start chirping and squawking back as Stan snaps his fingers:

"Awk……awk….awk………….awk……awk"

"awk……awk….awk………….awk……awk"

"awk……awk….awk………….awk……awk"

The crowd applauds.

"Folks never knew lizards could talk did you," says Stan.

Stan then heads back to their cages and the Gecko's run

back in.

"Those Geckos are something else. They were probably cursing me out!" says Stan as the crowd laughs.

Stand then opens another cage and pulls out some brown colored lizards that once again run over his shoulders.

"Now – these lizards like to lick their eyeballs because they have been sitting in dirt for awhile. Watch this:

Stan then turns to the lizards and starts rubbing his eyeballs as if he is wiping tears from his eyes. The lizard's tongues then shoot out from their mouths straight to their individual eyeballs and they lick….and lick….and lick!

The crowd oohs and ahhhs and laughs.

Stan then leads these lizards back to their cage.

"This last trick will completely blow your mind. These next lizards are known as "horned" lizards, also chameleons, and these animals do not play around, why you ask? These lizards eat mainly ants and other insects, but while they are eating breakfast or lunch of ants and mosquitoes or whatever, a bigger animal like a coyote may try to bother them – but the horned lizard doesn't play.

Stan heads to the last cage…. opens it up….and once gain these different lizards run across Stan's body. These lizards are brown…. horned…and mean looking.

Stan picks out just one of these lizards…. looks into its face….and says:

"You are an ugly looking monster – you ugly chameleon!"

The horned lizard shoots/squirts out a blood red liquid

directly into stan's face – very scary!!!"

Stan then wipes the red blood-stain from his face and shouts out into the audience "So you better not mess with these horned lizards.... all they are doing are protecting themselves. The blood it is shooting from its eyes is just to protect itself- kinda like a pepper spray. I ain't mad at him!"

Stan then moves his hands around and around……..and all the lizards from around his body.... run into various cages………and quicker than one can imagine ALL the lizards are back into their cages.

Stan moves to center stage – and takes a bow.

Treach & Tessa Treu Revue
Pee-Wee at center stage:

"Ladies and gentlemen, let's hear it for Stan the Lizard Man.... wasn't he amazing. We here at the Harlem Social Club never disappoint...we only bring you the best.

Next, coming to the stage is one of our greatest acts of the night.... of course, I'm talking about the great Treach and Tessa Treu Revue - who will bring you a faster music than the blues- this new music sweeping the country that combines blues with this new rhythm and blues and something even a little bit newer...something they are starting to label as "rock n' roll." This is the new music that the younger kids are getting into - but everybody should because it is original and you can really dance to it. I know you will love this new music, and I'm sure you fellas won't disagree that there are now more ladies moving on up and showing what the good Lord gave them. Let's just remember that these ladies - and we all - owe a great deal of respect and gratitude to those who graced this same stage and gave these new performers their platform - great women like Ethel Waters and Bessie Smith.... but the times they are a changing."

"So, ladies and gentlemen - without further ado - welcome to the stage the fantastic Treach and Tessa Treu Revue!"

The lights dimmed all around....and then a single light shone down from above to the middle of the closed curtain. Suddenly, a luscious, black women's leg popped out from the center stage curtain.... thigh high....... nothing but a beautiful black leg.

The audience went crazy wild!

Then - without the stage yet opening....... a funky drum beat started it off...a slow drum beat...then bass guitar riffs filled the ballroom...funky, slow bass riffs.... then guitar riffs....... then some horns joined in.... and as soon as it was getting good and loud-the music slowed back to the original slow beats? – as the stage curtain opened up.

Tessa Treu was the owner of that first luscious leg as she was the first one out once the curtains fully opened – with 2 equally luscious/dancers singers behind her. All 3 were dressed in short, skin-tight dresses that accented their curves at every turn.

The two back-up singers were s l o w l y swaying............ and popping......both their hips along with their long finger tips....... with the slow beat at the moment. Tessa then moved up front. She gracefully moved to the center/middle of the stage. With her luscious red lips glowing, she slowly began this rap:

"So now we are going to start off doing something slow and mellow – something nice and easy -you understand what I'm saying

But then we are gonna kick it up – and get funky and real

See – we will never do anything nice and easy to the end

the music will kick in and we will move into some rough stuff

we plan on blowing your minds:"

Tessa then rapped:

"'When I was just a little girl

 growing up

All we did was work in the fields

didn't even have a pup

My daddy and mom said that's just the way it be

But they told me one day maybe when I got older

I could help myself and be free

So….as I grew and got older

I did get out of those fields and discovered I could sing

And I love my mom and pops

But my joy is my voice and the songs it brings

So Harlem Duke - I hope you enjoy what you are about to hear

Cause we don't shortchange - we play with all we got - no fear!

Background girls:

"Rolling…. Rolling…. rolling down the valley

"Rolling…Rolling…. rolling ever happy

Tessa - now singing:

'When I was just a little girl, just working in the fields

My momma said - girl, you know you can get a better deal

But I never understood exactly what she was trying to say

Until I started to sing and my mind turned from white to gray"

Girls:

"You are a proud mary lady – go ahead and be your queen

Nobody cares about your past - be yourself.... just be seen

Let it all loose- sing and dance like nobody looking

Free your mind, be bad Tessa- you the queen of cooking

(The band kicks it up a notch – a little louder and quicker)

Tessa – rapping again:

So, we want to bring you something a little bit harder.... meatier...

So, pick it up band......let's get a little more grittier

Cause life is not easy – you got to learn to take the good with the bad

If life was perfect and nothing ever went wrong – you wouldn't know the word sad

Sit back and listen....... and allow us to entertain you

Cause we are a special band in the land- the Treach and Tessa Treu Revue!"

The band really started rolling. The horns (trumpet, sax, and trombone) picked up, as well as the keyboards and bass. Treach was on guitar, and he really started to bring it – singing:

"Just rolling.......rolling.....rolling down the valley

("I said we are just rolling")

I said we are just rolling...rolling...rolling down the valley

(he held that last VALLEY)

The back-up girls and Tessa then spun around two or three times as the new highlighted music kicked in....and the crowd went wild! The band was kicking wild – and Tessa and the girls were twirling and whirling and kicking unlike Diddley had ever seen. The back-up girls had their wigs flying in their faces – while Tessa had her short bob nice and sweet over her face- it was quite the contrast.

The band played 3 fast songs....as the girls and the band broke out into tremendous sweats as they were laying it all out – giving it their all like Didd had never witnessed. Treach's band was hopping and skipping, while not missing a funky beat.

Finally – Tessa threw her hand in the air with one finger pointed up. The band hit that one last note:

KABOOM!

The crowd exploded in extended applause....... raised the roof it was so loud with their handclaps, whistles, and foot stomping!

What a performance.... whew.

Diddley was astounded, as he watched from the side of the stage, as Treach and Tessa finished their fabulous show. Didd reflected a bit, and thought maybe this was the **best professional act he had seen to date?** Tessa just gave it her all – in her short hair – and she really, really seemed like she was different and relieved when she was on the stage as opposed to when they first met and had their first conversation. Once she was on the stage – she transformed herself to the moment and gave it her best. It was a moment that Diddley would never forget!

As they exited the stage, Tessa made a special moment to come over to Diddley and offer him some advice:

"Just give it your all Mr. Diddley Squatt – play from your heart. You can only do the best you can do – so don't be afraid to let your light shine. Say a little prayer before going on stage….and you light them up Mr. Diddley."

She gave Diddley a sweaty hug – and Didd was completely frozen….no response. Treach came through first smiling – but he pushed Tessa after seeing her hug Diddley, Strange? – Diddley thought?

TREACH LOOKED DIRECTLY DEEP INTO DIDDLEY'S FACE WITH THE MEANEST GROWL DIDD HAD EVER WITNESSED – BUT NO WORDS WERE EXCHANGED.

Pee-Wee was at center stage quickly:

"NOW I KNOW YOU LIKE TREACH TREU AND ESPECIALLY TESSA AND THE GIRLS – AM I RIGHT ABOUT IT"

Crowd: 'YEAH!!!!"

"Next we have for you a different kind of act. There aren't a lot of black opera singers in the Unites States, but coming to the stage is the anomaly in that field. Let's hear an operatic masterpiece by none other than Madam Dorethea Doolidge."

Dorethea Doolidge

Curtain opens:

In the center of the stage is this older black woman. With just one look, it was easy to ascertain that once upon a time……. possibly/probably many years ago……. when she was younger, this lady was undoubtedly a drop-dead beautiful woman – one could just sense it on first glance. However, as with us all, father time had taken its diligence - and one could see that age had taken its toll to her face, her skin, her hair………. her wrinkles. Her body showed the rigors of traveling and painful unknowingness of constant uncertainty………. of moving from one city to the next on a night's notice. Her eyes were wrinkled and although she was by no means a heavy woman – her cheeks were jowled and tanned a deep brown.

Dorethea wore her hair in a simple pulled back ponytail that fell upon her neck and the top of her back. It was a simple do – probably because it was a cheap way for upkeep and she probably had one of the girls on the bus pull it back for her before each show….no need for a paid-for stylist like some of the other headliners.

It suddenly hit Diddley, while presently watching as Dorethea prepared for her song, that he indeed remembered seeing her earlier on the bus. She sat to the right rear, alone, shielding her face from the sun as it shone through the window, and while other folks were joking and laughing and talking – Dorethea sat alone unsmiling and just looking out the window. HOWEVER- the one difference noticed about Dorethea – was while she did not have anyone sitting next to her……there was indeed a **cat cage** sitting up right there in the seat? Dorethea would from time-to-time lean over and whisper to her cat – and this would bring the only smiles to her face. So that's what Diddley knew- which was very little - about this next act:

There stood Dorethea in a black dress – center stage –

wearing a black dress with a red sage crossed over her neck.

Then the band broke into a slow, melancholy music of the type Diddley had never heard before. This music was formal and basic, highlighted by the various stringed instruments (the guitarist had actually picked up a violin?) and a standing bass....it sounded unlike music Diddley had ever heard before? Dorethea started singing and it was unlike any other sound ever heard in the auditorium and it was nothing but respect.

"Nessun dorma! Nessun dorma!
Tu pure, oh Principessa
Nella tua fredda stanza
Guardi le stelle che tremano
D'amore e di speranza

Ma il mio mistero è chiuso in me
Il nome mio nessun saprà
No, no, sulla tua bocca lo dirò
Quando la luce splenderà
Ed il mio bacio scioglierà
Il silenzio che ti fa mia"

"What is this?" Sly heard Diddley say.

"You ninny,' said Sly, "she is definitely singing in a different language. Even we animals can recognize that there are different languages.? Jesus...and they say humans are the smartest specie?"

Dorethea's second verse was in English:

"Nobody shall sleep!...
Nobody shall sleep!
Even you, oh Princess,
in your cold room,
watch the stars,
that tremble with love and with hope.

> But my secret is hidden within me,
> my name no one shall know...
> No!...No!...
> On your mouth, I will tell it when the light shines.
> And my kiss will dissolve the silence that makes you mine!...
> (No one will know his name and we must, alas, die.)
> Vanish, o night!
> Set, stars! Set, stars!
> At dawn, I will win! I will win! I will win!"

As Dorethea sang each verse, the stage spotlight from above hit directly in her face at specific intervals, to highlight the contortions attributed to each octave necessary for this dramatic song, as she sang high and low – jowls exasperated - GIVING IT HER ALL. Dorethea swung her arms for various verses, accenting what she was singing. Now, although the crowd may not have none the Italian words she sang - all could easily *feel* the meaning of the word – because of the emphasis she put forth.

It was majestic!

"My God!" said Diddley as Sly ran upon his shoulders, "this lady is majestic! I have never heard this song before, or the language it was sang, but I feel its power.......... opera must be a very popular field of music for many people – the power of the music."

"Now you are talking some sense my friend," said Sly squirreling about," that's why music brings people together. Music doesn't need words....... all it needs is a chance and a feeling. There is room for us all – that's what I've been trying to preach to my animal friends- but they are still afraid of you humans.

Dorethea then finished the last verses of Nessun Dorma with an auditorium, body-shaking shrill note that had everybody in the funky Harlem Duke Social Club on their feet clapping unlike anything else Diddley had ever witnessed before!

Doreathea walked off after this **one song.... that's all she** did was one song.... but that one song was enough. I guess black folks had their opera queen!

As Dorethea exited the stage to an astounding standing ovation – after just her one song- Diddley ran up to her and shook her hand. Diddley helped her down from the stage:

"Miss Dorethea Doolidge, I have never, ever......ever.... heard such a soul-searching song before in my life! I am just starting out on the Chitlin Circuit Tour- but I want you to know I am an "eclectic" person and I love all kinds of music. I was born and raised in Rundown, Mississippi, and I have never heard an opera song until just know. It was fantastic!

"Thank you Mr. Diddley Squatt; I appreciate your sincere words. I have been fortunate enough to live into my 70's – please recognize that a real woman never reveals her age – but I can pass along that this thing called "music" helps provide universal life. My young friend, please understand that God put "difference" into each part of life for a purpose – I'm talking about all different forms of creation you see around you....the key is "difference" - whether it be human, animal, plant, stars – different ; or people – black, white, yellow, brown - different; food – greens, yellow-squash, pumpkin, noodles, beans - different; religion – Baptist, Muslim, Presbyterian, protestant, Jewish - different; sizes- big, tall, fat, slim - different; women...men – different. So, why should music be any different? Blues, jazz, country, opera – different. My advice to you is to just celebrate it all and don't hold back, but I think you know this already. I am surprised you used the word "eclectic" in your first words to me – you are the youngest soul I've ever heard recite that word. It is also one of my favorites – Sir Diddley."

"So, I am indeed glad to meet a kindred soul who likes all different forms of music and is willing to listen first before judging. Opera is one of the oldest forms of music, and it is easy to see how it has survived all these years – it can be sung in any language and one can still understand what is being said. My good friend, I'm sure we will have future discussions about music and please know you can always come to me with any questions about anything. Now I need to get my rest."

And with that Diddley helped her down from the stage and some handlers then took over to take Dorethea to her dressing room. It was indeed a first meeting Diddley would never forget!"

As she left, it was again time for Pee-Wee:

"Wasn't that great ladies and gentlemen.... opera on the Chitlin Circuit. Management loves bringing "different" to you folks – and especially if it is performed by somebody classy and brassy – and as you all just witnessed- who is brassier that Dorethea Doolidge. Thank you Darling.

"Now…………………………………………………………
Ya'll ready for some laughs?

Crowd: "yeah!"

"Well then get ready to grab your sides and hitch them stitches……cause we got none other than the funniest man, I don't care either black, white, yellow, brown, purple ----- alive, coming to the stage next. Harlem Duke…. welcome none other than Slappy Fox!"

Comedian Slappy Fox Performance

"Hey………. how is all my negroes doing out there? My name is Slappy Fox and I'm what is called a comedian…for all you ladies, my name comedian means that first I "come" and then "didn't" I leave!

(laughter)

"But really – I'm just here to entertain y'all and hopefully shed some fun on this crazy world we are living in today. Negroes-we are living in some crazy times! Black folks are trying their best to assimilate into society – and uplift our black people - but many white folks and maybe some of y'all even don't even now what "assimilate" means.

Well...to black folks.... especially to a man and a woman – assimilate means:

Black Meaning: black man in bed (looks at his watch): "Girl- I been waiting...is your "ass" ready to simulate me?'

White Meaning: white man in bed (looks at his watch): Beautiful girl – I am ready to "assim to the lake" with you and have a ball!"

(laughter)

"Now – your Slappy Fox boy here loves him some women. But I want to tell the men out there – you have to be careful when dealing with women.... they are some different creatures then us men. They can drive you to drink! I remember when I met and married my first wife- I been married 5 times – but when I met and married my first wife. She was a cab driver – and the best thing she ever did for me – was drive me to get my drinks - cause she was definitely driving me crazy!"

(laughter)

And that was only my first wife. I got a lot of stories to tell you about my various wives....and unfortunately the stories ain't all good. Take my second wife – please take her!

(Laughter)

"See.... I was walking down the street with my second wife in North Carolina one night after we went to the show, and this negro dude ran up from behind us and shoved a gun in my back and said "Your money or I'm taking your life!"

I was frightened but happened to say "what you say?"

He said, "I said give me all of your money or I'm taking your life."

I told him "I've lived a good life so far...I really don't care if you take my life."

He looked at me like I was crazy – then turned to my wife, then turned back to me, and said – 'OK nigger – you think I'm playing....... if you don't give me all your money right now – I'M TAKING YOUR WIFE!" I thought about it a minute, and then I said:

"OK you win – I'm not giving you anything – MY WIFE IS YOURS."

(laughter almost brought the house down.)

"Oh lord...let me ask y'all.... what's the difference between a pickpocket and a peeping Tom? A pickpocket snatches watches – while a peeping Tom watches snatches!"

(there was a delay...but then when folks let it resonate a bit – laughter)

"My negro folks...these is some crazy times. I walked into a restaurant in Mississippi not too long ago after having a little too many drinks at this negro bar – I wasn't paying attention – but I was hungry and wanted a piece of pie or something – as I said, I wasn't paying attention. So, I walked in, and there was this white woman waitress, who was ugly by the way, she was behind the counter, and I said "what kind of pie do you serve here?"

She said "You must not have seen the sign," and then pointed to a sign that we've all seen before – it read:

"WE DON'T SERVE COLORED PEOPLE HERE."

So, I said…" That's OK…I don't eat colored people…but I do likes me some pie!" Shit…. took me 3 days to get out of jail!"

(laughter)

Diddley and Sly were mesmerized by Slappy Fox as neither had ever seen a black comedian live. It really helped loosen Diddley up and he thought to himself of how the Chitlin Circuit was more than just a performance venue and a way of life for those in the upper management areas to make money, but also a chance and an outlet for black performers from the street, like him - both beginners and long-timers, to showcase their talents and to gain a following – and for many – just to make some money and put food on the table.

Diddley shook Slappy Fox's hand as he left the stage.

"Good luck youngblood. I really hope you do good on your first performance on this tour……. I remember when I first did my break-in many years ago how terrified I was when I first took the stage. That's why I didn't do any jokes about your name – "Diddley Squatt" – cuz I want you to do good. But young blood – you can bet on your next performance I'll have a joke a two about "Diddley Squatt?"

Didd and Slappy both slapped hands and laughed at Slappy's comment – it was a nice and sincere good luck wish.

Pee-Wee was back center stage:

"Ladies and gentlemen…. have you been entertained?"

Crowd: "YES"

"Well get ready to be entertained for some terrific dancing by a world class dancer. This guy overcame losing a leg at an early age but he still had the urge and nerve to tell the world "you can't stop me from dancing." So, for all you Saturday night folks who like to lindy-hop or shake that top when you hear the jive- let's bring to the stage the one and only Jack Leg Batey!"

Jack Leg Batey

The curtain opened and at center stage stood Jack Leg Batey. Jack was also a light skinned black-man, with tightly cropped hair that was receding in the front. He wore a tan suit and white shirt with a red bow-tie. He was in good shape – except for the slight leaning to the left side, due to he was missing his right leg! He wore pants that fully covered his left – but they were cut off at mid-thigh on his right leg – like shorts, instead of his leg, he had a wooden-stump-like peg with a metal spike sticking out at the bottom – kind-of like what Diddley remembers seeing on the arms of some pirates in pirate comic books when he was growing up – but Peg Leg's stump was on his right leg.

Peg-Leggy, or sometimes just called Pegey, spoke at center stage:

"Before I begin my performance, I would like to briefly tell you a little bit about myself. I was born Jack Manesha Batey in Marianna, Arkansas. I was one of the youngest of ten children born to Aquifah Norman and Loqacious Batey. My parents were sharecroppers who worked on the famous South Port Peter Brumsfield Cotton Fields way back in the day. We lived in the workers quarters and our parents worked in the cotton fields picking cotton from sun-up to sun down. As kids, we ran barefooted around our shanty house and played on the dusty roads. When we got old enough, we also worked in the fields.

We loved dancing, and for some reason, I was the best dancer in the neighborhood……. I could make my body move like nobody else.

One day me and some of my brothers were throwing a ball back and forth near one of the cotton gins where we lived and this white foreman yelled:

"Hey……. you little pick-a-ninnies need to get out of that area – can't believe I'm saying this – but it might be dangerous. That cotton gin machine is powerful and can catch you and throw you in. Get your asses out of there and go someplace else."

We laughed and my brother Willie said:

"That old fool can't tell us what to do…....but let's move on cause we don't want to get Ma and Pa in trouble. Hey Jack – let me see you catch this one last ball."

He threw it and it landed in the bottom of this barrel attached to this machine. Hell…. I didn't know what a gin machine was? So, I stepped into the bottom of this barrel to get the barrel and before I knew it I heard this grinding sound and this machine came to life. I was able to pull my left leg out, but this damn machine with these bottom teeth like things were on my leg and I screamed in pain:

"AAAAHHHHHHHHH   MY LEG!!!!!!!!"

The next thing I remembered was I woke up in my bed, and as I opened my eyes, my mother and father and all my sisters were over the top of me- and this white doctor, dressed all in white, told me they couldn't save my leg and it had to be "amputated." That's right- they had to chop off my leg. Everybody was crying……and I looked down and saw a blank spot where my leg should have been. I was too scared to say anything.

I remember I stayed in the hospital for about a month. Then a couple of doctors came in and I remember one particular doctor, I remember him because…strangely…he was negro…..his name was Dr. Strickland, said something like, "Mr. and Mrs. Batey, your son will need a prosthetic leg if he ever wants to learn how to get around and care for himself. But I'm sorry to tell you that such a leg is probably more expensive than you can afford. From the past, I know that some negro people have actually improvised and been able to make their own legs from other items such as discarded metals or wood stumps."

My father then said:

"My brother Hughey somehow learned how to carve wood when he was a little boy……I'm sure he can carve him some sort of leg out of wood. Mr. Doctor Strickland – we don't have any money, but I'm asking you if you would……ah………… if Hughey could carve him a leg – would you help with the next steps to make sure it fits and this boy can learn to walk again?"

"I would be glad to help with these next steps," said the doctor.

"That's why I remember his name – because he was a nice doctor and helped me…. Dr. Strickland.

So…before trying on any stumps, I used crutches to get around. For some reason – it was easy for me. I was walking around on one leg with the crutches…and actually dancing with the crutches.

The next step -my Uncle Hughey went to work. He first measured my leg from my stump to the ground- compared it to my left leg to insure it was balanced and equal – and Hughey made me my first stumps. For his first try, Hughey took a tree stump and crafted a leg-part that Dr. Strickland helped him tie to my stump- and it wouldn't come off. I got up and walked – and it felt good! The stump was round at the top to fit around my thigh, and then carved down at the end into a sharp square peg at the bottom. Dr. Strickland gave Uncle Hughey ideas if he wanted to change stuff up, and believe me Hughey did! Rest in peace Uncle Hughey, he made them as I grew and grew.

Then….and this is the most important part. Uncle Hughey and everybody knew I liked to dance. As I learned to walk with the crutches and the stump – stomping my stump felt like something natural to do. I would tap a crutch (Pegey then reached out and tapped an imaginary crutch against the floor and the drummer hit his bass drum for a "thump thump" right on time)- then tap my good leg (Pegey did a "tap ta'" with his good leg show which had a metal tap attached to the bottom") – and lo and behold- with my stump leg I was able to get a good sound (Pegey does a rhythmic tap with his peg-leg.) In no time at all – I found that my wood stump could manage MORE WEIGHT AND STRESS THAN MY REGULAR LEG! (Pegey does a full quick tap dance alternating the sequence with his good and stump leg.) My dancing became easy and very rhythmic. I started tapping my stump leg and it made a great sound. In no time I was dancing on street corners with an old rickety bucket out for any tips/change, and in barbershops, cafes – then, as I got older, in nightclubs. I was beginning to bring home more money than my parents were bringing home.

(the crowd erupts in laughter and applause)

Alright....... you've heard enough about my life. Let's get tonight started with some   dancing.......... drummer – give me a beat!"

The drummer then hit a wicked beat and Jack Leg Batey was off and running. Diddley couldn't believe his eyes, and Sly was just as excited. Diddley was the only one on his side of the backstage – so Sly felt free and exposed himself – dancing back n' forth across Diddley's shoulders imitating Jack's every step – even stopping to tap his right paw whenever Jack Leg Batey hit his.

Jack would dance with his good left leg and bang it on the wooden floor with strict force as the metal tap caromed off the banquet hall walls- then he would spend the same amount of time and bang his wooden right-leg stump – which also featured on the bottom a metal tap-product – the same damn beat. Jack would twirl................ .... slide....... He would fly across the room, tapping and twirling and hopping – like a butterfly with a sledgehammer on its feet.

He danced all around the stage and the audience loved it. He ended his show by requesting the music stop – and when it did- in the quite auditorium – it was just he and his magical legs and feet dancing on the floor. He did about 2 minutes of just tapping in rhythm. It was something!

It was very impressive….and when he said "thank you and god bless for watching me perform" – the crown rose and gave him a standing ovation.

"That was fantastic!" said Sly as the curtains closed so Sly ran to his pouch - and Jack Leg hopped off the stage, clicking his heels and stump galore. As he neared Diddley, he got directly in his face and offered the following words:

"Young Man – it is my tradition to offer first timers some advice - based upon my experience on being in this business for waaaaaaaaaaaaaay too many years. I can only tell you to always do your best and don't shortchange the customers who have paid to watch you perform. It is common sense. The promoters make money, but the customers have no control over the price of the ticket; no control over what is going on in your life and maybe any struggles you are going through; no control over anything but their choosing to come see you perform and give them some relaxation and a good time in their lives for at least one night. So never short-change them. Give it your all…and also – DON'T FORGET TO ENJOY YOURSELF! You are making a living performing, while they are working in the fields or a mill or a warehouse – you understand what I'm saying."

"I do sir…and I really appreciate your words" said Diddley, "your words are similar to what my Grandma Momma-Squatt and all the others have told me from the beginning – to just be true to myself, to respect every living thing, and to give it my best. However, these words, coming from someone who is an experienced performer in the very business I am trying to put my foot in – these words ring especially true. I appreciate them Jack Leg Batey – and I hope to make you proud one day," said Diddley.

Jack was shocked.

"Oh, my goodness? Such a nice and respectful young man you are," he said while patting Diddley on the back, "I can foresee only good things in your future. I will follow your career young Diddley Squatt. Play your music young gun!" and then he was gone into the back toward the dressing rooms.......Didd could hear his stomp hitting the floor after each other step.

"Clomp"........"Click"...................."Clomp"............"Click."

And Jack Leg Batey was gone.

Pee -Wee/MC Little hit the stage once again:

"How about that show ladies and gentlemen? The great Peg Leg Batey and his wonderous dancing skills. You've just witnessed one of the greatest dancers of all time – so remember this date.

Next, coming to the stage, is one of the greatest blues singers – or as we like to call them "crooners" – of all time. I am of course talking about the great Sam Bluester. This man really needs no introduction. He has bestowed us with some of the greatest blues songs of all time such as "Saturday Night is Alright for Dancing," "You My Little Cupid Blues," and "Let's Dance the Night Away Honey Child." Tonight......Mr. Bluester will start off with maybe his biggest hit of all time. Ladies and gentlemen, the World Famous Chitlin Tour proudly presents the amazing Sam Bluester as he sings his biggest hit of all time, "I was Born by the Lake." Take it away Sam.

SAM BLUESTER

The curtain opens and there stands the infamous Sam Bluester. He is dressed impeccably: black suit, white shirt, black-and-white patent leather shoes – and a red-bow tie.

"Ladies and gentlemen – I want to begin with a song I wrote too too many years ago, but it has managed to withstand the test of time. It is my main message to every living soul. I am so happy this is my legacy song:"

The drummer gave a drum roll……. the piano chimed in…. then the stand-up bass…. then the horns. A crescendo was reached and then there was silence for a second. S I L E N C E

Then Sam's voice roared:

"I was born by the lake

In a tiny patch

Whoa……. life was not easy then

And it hasn't been easy – ever since

It's been a long……. long road to travel

But i know deep in my heart – and it's still running

A change is a coming- oh yes- a change is round the bend

Oh lord---when i drop to my knees…. Everynight

I say lord....oh lord....please help me please

I'm trying to help my brothers and sisters, as much as i can

But this world is so tough – i need to know if it's in your plans

I just know, i will never give up and stop trying to be me

Just oh lord – just help us all get off our knees

So yes- i was born by this strange lake

In a little tiny patch

But i will never stop singing or pleading

I will always sing my songs, so listen to me and watch

It's been a long, l o n g time coming

But i know

A change is a coming.......and on that i won't repent!"

    Sam continued his song.......moving easily around the stage as he sang various verses....and Diddley couldn't help but notice many of the OLDER women in the auditorium raising their hands and shouting "hallelujah" that Diddley remembers from his many Sunday mornings in church.

    Sam did a couple of more songs – but like much of the other

Chitlin Circuit performers who were getting up in age and at their best were good for touring for maybe a couple of more years and could still spit out 3 or 4 songs a performance, that was about as much as they could handle. Sam sang a last song............told the crowd "God bless you and thanks for supporting black artists on this important tour" – and he was gone.

Of course, when Sam exited, he noticed Diddley standing on stage near the stage exit.

"Mr. Squatt, I noticed you stayed and watched my entire performance," said Sam as he stepped in front of Diddley. "I deeply appreciate you staying and watching my entire set. Whenever a performer performs, he always notices certain audience members and he can tell those who are really paying attention – and I saw that in you."

"No Mr. Bluester – it is I who needs to say "thank you" for allowing me backstage....... for allowing me on this tour.......to witness this closely the majesty of how you perform and give to your audience. You can bet I was making mental notes of how you moved about the stage, and interacted with your audience; how you gave everything while you were on stage. The honor was all mine and I give you the honor sir."

"Well, I am impressed with my old self- thank you young man for such great words!" said Sam as he reached and hugged Diddley, "I can't remember hearing such heartfelt words from such a young person nowadays. I am going to go in the back-dressing room and sit a quick spell, but then I am going to make sure I get my old ass up and come see you perform. Just remember, we performers must stick as a team and support each other," said Sam as hugged Diddley one last time and gave him an acknowledging wink as he kept moving and was gone to the stairs.

Wow! After talking to Sam Bluester, Diddley removed his electric guitar from his gig bag and plugged it into the amp just behind the curtain. Didd knew tonight was special and he had to perform special. Tonight, he wouldn't be playing anything on his acoustic. Tonight - was for playing and blowing people's minds!

IT WAS TIME!

Diddley stood backstage behind the curtains in his best/latest/most comfortable performance garb (faded blue jeans, with patches; a t-shirt with the slogan "LONG LIVE ROBERT JOHNSON" written across the chest; medium sized-afro.... tennis shoes.....and of course his sunglasses hung around his neck,) behind the curtain, while MC Little was up front talking about different advertisers and the process of all those promoting the Chitlin Circuit.

Sigh................ Diddley couldn't help but think back to all those who helped him get to this moment right here....first off his grandmother Momma Squatt; next, the girls of the Copp-A Squatt Inn who helped raise him (Delilah, Chastity, Tiffany the Epiphany, Destiny); then came some of the kids he met at school (Sabrina Tuggars, Pryor Richards, Marco Valentus, Glorendous); and those customers/characters who frequented the Copp-A-Squatt (Robert Johnson, Nate the Skate, Stew the Harmonica Fool ; and how could he ever forget his animal friends (Percy Possum, LadyMBug) along with his current best friend in life- Sir Sly!

Diddley bowed his head and said a silent prayer to himself.

Prayer:

"Thank you, God, almighty for my life to this point, and I hope to do some good in this world with your help. Thanks for all those I have met along the way because I wouldn't be here today, on this stage, if not for the friendships and lessons they have all taught me. I hope I do you all justice and maybe one day others will learn from my story. And as is told in one of my favorite Bible verses taught to me by my beloved Grandma Squatt – Psalm 86:11 –

"Teach me your way, O Lord, that I may walk in your truth; give me an undivided heart to revere your name - Amen."

Diddley then checked all the cords running from his guitar to the huge amplifier behind him. Most important was Didd's newest contraption called a wah-wah peddle – that was just invented recently - which when Diddley stepped on the peddle and gently rocked his foot up and down, while simultaneously strumming/plucking his guitar – would emit a funky "WANG WANG TWANG" sound that electrified the profound sling of the guitar strings. Diddley luckily had found the wah-wah peddle in a pawn shop that some musician desperately needed money and pawned it (which was a norm.)

He was ready…..finally, came the voice of MC Little:

Diddley Squatt

"Ladies and Gentlemen, tonight is a very special night indeed here at the World-Famous Harlem Duke Social Club, because tonight we have performing for you a special young cat who we are predicting will one day take the musical world by storm. Tonight, on this stage, will be the first major performance by a young guitar genius and maestro- who happens to go by the name Diddley Squatt."

(laughter throughout the club……. murmurs of "Did he say Diddley Squatt?" ……. more muted but polite laughter.)

"Now, I know that's kind of a different name, but Diddley is a different cat……. just give the young boy a chance, OK? So………without further ado – let's welcome to the world stage young Diddley Squatt!"

(Applause and laughter…. laughter and applause.)

The stage curtains pull open and there stands Diddley, alone on stage, with just his guitar wrapped around his shoulder.

Did awkwardly steps to the microphone:

"I'm.......... I'm......I'm not much for words, I prefer playing music over talking.... but I do want to say thank you for coming out tonight to listen to these great blues performers. I am one blessed, honored, and a lucky young dude to be standing up here where such past great and famous performers that have performed. In just our quick meetings, I love all the performers on this tour who I've known for only a short time, and I feel so blessed. I will do my best to bring you what I hear in my heart...that's about all any artist can do. With that, this is an original song I wrote called "Purple Phrase."

Diddley then steps back and plucks his guitar and the first lick is almost deafening it is so loud. Some in the crowd put their hands over their ears. As the riff is rounding to the end, Didd steps on his wah-wah peddle and he takes that one riff to new heights – LIKE HIS GUITAR IS CRYING:

"waaaaaayyyyyyyyyyyyyyyyyyyyy whyyyyyyyyyyyyyyyyyyyyyyyyyyyyyyyywowwwwwwwww wwwwwwwwwwwwwwwwwwwwwwwwwwwwwwwwwww wwaaaaayyywaaayyyyyth:"

The crowd is mesmerized...they had never heard a song start off with just a single guitar lick....and what was this wah-wah contraption they probably thought?

Silence...and then Didd broke into a funky beat jam as he sang:

"Purple phrase, all in my head

Wake me up – no time to be dead

Acting funny, and I don't seem shy

Scuse me – while I soar and fly

Purple phrase, whatcha gonna say

Keep on living, for at least another day

Acting funny, and it's not a joke

Make your money – gonna never be broke

Did then left his center stage area and moved to the left of the stage, while churning out some never before heard type of guitar licks……. just shredding his fingers from the top of the guitar (with a lower sound) – to the middle area – (and a mid- level range) to the bottom level of the guitar where the licks were in the higher range and it was like the guitar was singing in pain!

Back to center stage moved Diddley:

"Purple phase………..no need to refrain

Life is in the heart, maybe a little in the brain

So, keep on living good, and don't be shy

Scuse me- while my guitar and I fly!

Didd then moved to the RIGHT front of the stage, and tore into guitar licks to ensure those in the middle, left, and right of the club got a chance to see and hear him as he shredded and beat his guitar like he promised Robert Johnson one day he would.

This was indeed Diddley's positive comeuppance – his chance to showcase his unique skills and show any doubters that he was sincere in his music.

He stood there to the right of stage and just went up and down his guitar. The audience is front of him had never heard any such fast...then slow....then high...then low......sounds coming from this new electric guitar instrument. Didd then moved his guitar to his head and lips – and actually lipped some guitar licks! The audience was totally dumbstruck. Didd them moved back to the center microphone for the last phrases of his song:

"Purple phrase....... it's God's gift to us all

Ain't nobody perfect, we all gonna fall

But the key is to get up and uplift, and never quit your desire,

Cause a Purple phrase, is not a smokescreen – It is a definite fire! "

Diddley then stepped back.... Slung his guitar around his neck and the guitar swung 3 times....... he caught it on its fourth twirl – grabbed the neck – did fell to the floor and did the splits:

End of song.

Didd raises his arms into the air.......... expecting to hear some grand applause and claps and cheers from the exhilirated audience............ except????????????...............there vis dead.......... dead silence? Didd stands there all alone....... center stage.... looking out into the crowd..
.....and all there is - is exactly nothing...

............................*DEAD SILENCE*...............................

probationary

............................*DEAD*

SILENCE... ... ...

... ...DEAD SILENCE... ... ...

Finally.. words from the audience that those sitting backstage could hear. Diddley still center stage – still silence- so he could also hear:

Men

(Older black man):

"Nope. Don't get it. Stick to the blues or jazz…. this will never catch on! And what in the world was he wearing with those blue jeans and what they call them – tennis shoes?"

(Middle age black man):

"That boy is strange……but his strangeness is interesting….but not for now?

(Younger black boy):

"What the Squatt was that? …wow,,,,,,,,,,,,,I loved it…. but…….er…….I better not let my parents know I kinda loved it or they will throw me outta the damn house! Where can I get me some blue jeans?"

Women

(Older black woman):

"I don't know what the hell that was – for a debut on the Chitlin Circuit? I guess he was intentionally unique. But to tell you the truth – I HATED IT?"

(Middle aged black woman):

"These youngsters trying to put out this new electric music? Ain't having it -just stick to the blues- that's all we need!"

(Young black woman):

"Oh my...that was indeed different. But my god- that diddley squatt boy is so cute – and has such a beautiful face and the sweetest dimples – i'm a hafta watch out for him (giggles galore!)"

(various):

"I like his new music...why should we always have to hear about the blues and how tough times are. Shit- don't nobody have to remind me I live it every-day. I want some positive music and hope in this life. This young boy seems like he understands that!"

(various): "I don't know. That sound is too damn loud.... but I do like what he was wearing and singing about......I'll reserve my full judgement until I see him again.........he was very handsome.... but he ain't ready yet!"

(various): "I didn't like it! We don't pay for this new stuff. Just give me some standard blues songs and get off the stage. I don't care about what's happening...give me my blues and let me go home and cook Charles his biscuits and gravy.... maybe Charles will treat me later on or not.... but I don't need this new stuff."

(Young black girl and brother siblings brought by their parents to their first ever concert);

"OH WEE............. We loves us some Diddley Squatt

better than all the other performers. Is this what we've been missing all these years? We love Diddley Squatt and his sanging and guitar playing."

The kid's parents then stood up and yelled at their kids:

"Shut up Quinesha and Jukee…. you kids don't know nothing about music. That Diddley boy's music was horrible!"

MC Little then yelled from the side of the stage:

"Diddley – sing your next songs – you gotta keep going!"

Diddley awoke from what he just heard….and sure enough, moved on to his next songs. He then played some blues standards taught to him by Robert (Bobby)Johnson.

At the end of his 45-minute set, Diddley moved to the microphone:

"That's it. I want to once again thank you all for once again listening to my music. I'm sorry if I disappointed some of you. I know it is different, but I love different. See – that first song I came out to was an original song I wrote – I just love this newer fast jazz/rhythm and blues that is coming out. When I was a young boy raised at the Copp-A-Squatt Inn in Rundown, Mississippi, I learned a new word from this famous blues musician you've undoubtedly heard of, by the name Robert Johnson – who once told me (didd moves into a raspy old voice)

"Youngblood……..my best advice to you is to be an "eclectic" person. Have you ever heard the word "eclectic?" Eclectic is my favorite word- Eclectic means that you LISTEN TO EVERYTHING – NO PREJUDICE- AND THEN PICK OUT WHAT YOU LOVE – and don't worry what people think. If you like the blues…..play some blues. If you like jazz….play some jazz. If you like some country and western even – play you some country and western. And the key……..at some point – combine them all into what your heart hears- and then you have some new music. Shit…..don't listen to what people are saying….you only own your heart and your mind- you know what you like and let that light shine. Hell boy….be ECLECTIC AND NEW!"

"So…. thank you for listening to me….my name is proudly Diddley Squatt – Peace out!"

Didd exited the stage, throwing up two fingers in what looked like the letter "V"- it was a newly coined gesture meaning "PEACE."

As Diddley excited the stage he was surprised by the greetings he received. As he walked back toward the stage exit he turned to look at the audience and this is what he heard and saw:

MANY FOLKS STANDING AND BOOING…. SOME POINTING THEIR THUMBS DOWN IN A NEGATIVE FASHION…..SHOUTS OF:

"'You aint ready yet"

"what the hell was that!"

"all we want is the good old blues – none of this new stuff"

Although…..some of the younger patrons did stand and clap……….but overall…….IT WAS NOT A POSITIVE RESPONSE.

Diddley was heartbroken as he finally reached the back of the stage.

Sigh………………………………………………………….
………………………………………………………

This was actually the first time Diddley felt *real sadness in his heart area*. He had just sung his first original song – and obviously a lot of the folks (especially the oldtimers) didn't like it. It was one of the first/biggest negative experiences in his young life?

When he finally got to the backstage area and was heading for the door – there stood his fellow performers and you could tell many of them felt for Diddley…. but then again, they too probably had similar situations in their young careers……. their expressions and words were brief:

King. D.D. – "Don't worry – we all been thru similar stuff – life ain't always easy and peasy perfect, that's why even if a string breaks on your guitar – you still got four friends to help you finish what you started!"

Stand the Lizard Man – "Life has all kinds of animals – good and bad – there are beautiful butterflies in this world as well as nasty snakes."

Dorethea Doolidge – "You think people loved me singing opera when I first started……. I say to you "RIMANI FORTE E CORAGGIOSO" – which means stay strong and courageous in Italiano!"

Slappy Fox – "Hey youngblood – if my world were perfect, you think I'd be out here on this tour and about to get back on this bus?…shit………I'd be drinking champagne and sleeping with the Queen of England…of course my wife (which ever one – been so many- the one at the time) would find out and kill me the next day!"

Jack Leg Batey – "Remember – I once had 2 legs……but a leg lost doesn't mean you still can't stand strong!"

Sam Bluestar – "This is why the Blues was started and will always be around – life is ups and downs – but you always find the positive in both!"

Tessa Treu – "Of course we are here to support you…. you

think my life has been easy?"

Diddley nodded to them all and gave each performer a worthwhile nod of thanks as he moved toward the exit.......... he couldn't talk – but he felt a friendship like never before. As he got to the door and turned to head towards his room.......... of course, Treach was outside the door with a whiskey drink in his hand. Treach's words:

'How'd you like that response newbie diddley? Your new music ain't squatt.... go back to Mississippi and find a job working in the fields....your hands were made for picking cotton – not picking a guitar!"

Treach threw the glass against the wall and let out a guttural laugh as he stumbled down the hallway.... laughing uncontrollably.

HA........HA....................................HA......................
..............HA.......HA..

Diddley in his room.... sitting in his bed. Uncomfortable.... even Sly thought it was best to let him relax and meditate about what just happened. It was just one night?

Didd thought – maybe this is just the way the tour and life worked? – you had to keep moving in order to make any type of profit, money, or learn from an experience.

Didd alone with his thoughts. He took out his journal and started writing – just free writing the thoughts in his head on what had just transpired on this historic night.

He jotted down the words of encouragement from King D.D.; the take-a-ways from Stan the Lizard Man; the great performance from the Treach and Tessa Treu Revue and Tessa's words to him after the performance; Dorethea Doolidge, and how she exposed him to opera music and her words of encouragement in Italiano and how powerful different types of music can be; Slappy Fox – how funny was he?; Jack Leg Batey – how to never let any type of handicap stop you from pursuing your dream; Sam Bluester – an old blues singer who just loved perfecting his craft and entertaining folks.

At the end, Diddley wrote down I DID THE BEST I COULD DO.

Didd jotted down notes on all these areas…..he knew he would review them from time to time whenever he hit obstacles – but he had them in writing for actual reference.

He fell asleep with the journal in his hand…….no more words to write.

CHAPTER 5
Diddley Bonds with Mute

The next morning.

The excitement and disappointment from the night before was indeed fleeting, Didd quickly learned, because after his first historic performance the previous night - the night passes quickly my friend! The morn comes quickly and suddenly............sigh.

The rule on this particular Chitlin Circuit Tour was there was an unwritten order that the more experienced, older veteran entertainers had first choice to seats on the Betty-B as he/she moved down the tour route, i.e. the veterans were allowed first on the bus and got what seats they wished. Most of them preferred seats in the rear/back of the bus- because - hey – back there first off there was more leg room, but also you could more easily pass along your drink of choice, your smoke of choice, your whatever of choice – and nobody would mind. Made sense....so the more veteran performers ALWAYS took the back seats first.

This meant the "newbies" sat in the front, and Diddley was the "newbiest" of newbies.

So, there was Diddley, waiting along the side of the bus, when it was time to depart the Harlem Duke Club and move onward. Sly was of course in Didd's guitar pouch, the ever-observant passenger, excited to see what the haps would bring.

The first to board were members of the Treach and Tessa True Revue. Treach, who was sometime called Tre, himself was the first to board. Strange? While most of those moving on the bus were informally dressed in early morning gear of hastily thrown on pants and ragged shirts or jeans – some even in pajama bottoms and tops – Treach was eloquently dressed in a shirt and tie and sunglasses galore – and a wool like jacket wrapped around his shoulders that some of the girls made sure to keep tidy as he walked on with his trimmed suit and sunglasses. Didd thought "wow – these girls really looked after Treach," but he also wondered, if Tessa was his wife/girl – how could she allow such a scene? It was the first inkling to Didd that maybe stardom was special.

So, Treach and Tessa and them took all the rear seats.

Next, Stan the Lizard man came on board and while some of his lizards where in cages loaded into the back/bottom of the truck, Stan had a clause in his contract that his best/most important lizards could travel with him on the bus- in their special cages. As Stan got on, Mute got on after Treach and Tessa, and Stan's posse made it a point to stay a couple of seats in-front of them to not offend, so he kept his "babies" with him in cages that the crew was used to handling. From this gesture alone, Didd surmised that Stan was a very fair, calm man who mainly cared about his lizards and his business. Nuff said!

Next?

King D.D. boarded and was his royally majestic self. He didn't mind that although he and Dorethea may have been the elder/oldest members in the group – Treach and his bunch were far ruder and didn't abide by "obey your elders" and allow them on the bus first for their picks of seats.

"Don't mean a thing if it ain't got no sting!" said King D.D. with a chuckle and poked Didd on the side, "some of these younger acts don't get it and have the need to be courted and THINK they are on top. That's alright……King D.D. can sit anywhere on the bus, without a fuss – cause God is good and I can still walk, sing, and perform," he winked at Didd and climbed on board. Didd thought- what a gracious and kind soul King D.D. was? doesn't matter where he sits as long as he can still perform his best. Nice!

Dorethea came next and Didd made sure to go over and help her step up onto the bus steps.

'Thank you young man. I caught your act last night and was quite impressed. And as I mentioned, don't let anything negative get you down. Just remember to continue to be you, learn from us old folks, and reach out to those you don't know. That is God's way…..that………and a lot of soul…" she stepped up onto the bus.

"Wow" – Didd said to himself……." I like the oldsters better than the youngsters…..they seem so helpful."

"Of course – you nut" said Sly as he raised himself up for a moment, "didn't Momma Squatt tell you who would be the source of encouragement along the way? Old folks are the best………..geeessshhhhhhhh," as Sly ducked back into his pouch because Slappy Fox was approaching and Sly NEVER wanted to be caught off guard, but especially by a comedian who would roast him in a future act from claw to tail.

Slappy didn't waste any time as he saw Diddley at the door awaiting his turn:

"Hey young homie…..you got some talent on you…..don't let that reaction last night bother you…….just remember to be like my left toenail and to keep growing. And like my third, fourth, and fifth wives – never stop asking for help!"

Although Didd had just met most of the performers only days before – and he may have casual met some of them way back when they had ventured through the Copp-A- Squatt years earlier, he enjoyed just talking to them and how they reacted to him now that he was trying to do what most of them had been doing for countless years.

So Slappy was funny and nice….and Diddley appreciated his words.

Next came Jack Leg-Batey. He was of course dressed immaculately, and he hobbled but gently - and one may not have ever known he was missing a leg – that was Jack-Leg's apparently wish.

"Young man – keep on pushing,"" said Jack-Leg as Didd grabbed his arm and helped him onto the bus.

"Mr. Jack-Leg – you have no idea how impressed I was with your performance. You are truly professional, and it was just unbelievable how you performed and wanted people to appreciate your performance…. because you give stuff without a leg? I will never forget it – and you can bet whenever I step on stage, I will think of you and how fortunate I am to have my arms and legs – to play my guitar and move around….and here you are doing it missing a leg. It was something I will never forget."

"Great words of praise coming from such a young man," said Jack-Leg as he reached up and grabbed the bar to enter the bus. He stopped and looked down at Diddley.

"Just play your music from your heart young man…..just remember that the audience paid some money to see you perform – and that's all it takes. Give it your heart – and the rest will take care of itself. Thanks for helping me," were the words of Jack-Leg as he made it to the aisle of the bus and gentle moved on down.

The last to board was the most gracious - and even at this early hour in the morning - the stylishly dressed Sam Bluester! Sam was wearing a brown suit this morning, with glistening brown and white pumped shoes; a brown checkered handkerchief tucked ever so neatly in his upper left suit pocket, and a brown scarf wrapped around his neck area.

"Ahh……Mr. Squatt. How are you doing this fine morning?" said Sam.

"I'm doing fine Mr. Bluester," said Diddley as he extended and shook Sam's hand. "It was quite a night last night and I keep pinching myself to make sure I'm not dreaming. The reaction wasn't exactly what I was expecting – but I'll learn and move on."

"A pinch always does good young man – but I can tell you it was all true last night; including your amazing closing performance. If you listened to my final song last night it was entitled "I Was Born by the Lake."

"I loved that song," said Diddley, "it had some dynamite lyrics."

"Dynamite? That must be one of these new hip words you youngsters are throwing around," laughed Sam as he patted Diddley lovingly on his shoulder. "I'll have to remember that word and mention it to one of the songwriters I know for a possible song. Don't worry – I'll be sure to give you partial songwriter's credit."

"Cool," Diddley heard Sly murmur from his pouch.

Finally…after all the famous acts were on the bus- the last ACT was of course Diddley Squatt. Diddley stepped on, with his gig-bag slung over his shoulder and the unexposed Sly enclosed, and quickly took one of the seats up front – lucky to get a window seat…..although there were still some seats left in the back? Diddley turned around and looked around – just pinching himself that he was about to embark on the second leg of the world famous Chitlin Circuit. The next city would be the Carver Theater in Birmingham Alabama…..about a 6 ½ hour ride up north Alabama. As Diddley looked around the bus at different faces, he just thought about their prior night's performance and how now, the night before, it didn't seem to bother any of them if they had forgot lyrics or sang out of tune. Hey….this was a business – and on to the next show. By looking into their faces, Diddley could kind of tell maybe those who had stayed up until the wee hours and maybe "partied" a little bit too long? Treach Treu had on very dark sunglasses to hide his eyes – and it was hardly sunny outside – so that was a giveaway. King D.D……….Slappy Fox….Jack-Leg…….and MANY of the background singers and musicians were not as talkative this early in the morning, as they hung their heads or leaned against windows just glad to make it on the bus.

Diddley turned back around, and assumed it was time for the bus to depart when he saw W.C. climb his huge butt into the driver's seat. W.C. then grabbed the mike and said:

"For all my Chitlin Circuit performer folks, that was once again a great concert and a fantastic start, for most of y'all anyway, but now it is time to move on to another round of this next Chitlin concert. As always – before we depart, let's welcome on board the roadies and assistants that handle all the luggage; set up all the equipment; run errands – and who without them, this tour would not be possible…..welcome aboard the famous "CC CREW!"

Some cheered in the back – others said "whatever" – as the last remaining members of the crew came on board and filled the remaining empty seats – all up front of course. The seat next to Diddley was soon the only remaining open seat, so the roadie known as Mute sheepishly slid into the seat. He looked at Diddley with a look like "Are you O.K. with me sitting next to you?"

Diddley winked at Mute and made sure to slowly and carefully face him face-to-face, and mouth the words – "SURE OK" – knowing that Mute could read his lips, Diddley continued slowly:

"What's up Mute- glad you are sitting next to me. I definitely want to get to know you. Welcome aboard my friend," as he extended his hand and Mute hurriedly and excitedly shook his hand. Mute was dressed in his usually road-gear clothes surmised of blue-jean overalls, a dusty white t-shirt, red work boots, and a bandana tied around his head with his pulled back red hair and freckles all afresh. Mute had the greenest eyes, and actually great white teeth compared to other similar day workers at the time.

Mute slowly mouthed his response to Diddley…….very slowly……..while making these funny moves with his hands?

"Mr. Diddley-Squatt…..I was so glad to set up your gear – I told the rest of the workers that I specifically wanted to set up your stuff, because you were so nice to me the first time we met and I felt kind of a bond with you – I can't explain it – but I just had this feeling that you were a kind and understanding person. I could see it in your eyes. I get these feelings on only a few people in my life, and I certainly got this feeling upon my first meeting with you. And then, when I first heard you play……. from the first note……….I know that you are special and will make a name for yourself in this world, you just watch. Don't worry about those who booed last night – I've seen that before with new performers. I'm not wrong about this. People may think I'm dumb, stupid, and crazy, but you will see and one day look back on this day when we first talked about it."

Mute continued:

"So, you know I can't talk that well, although I can make sounds similar to words I am trying to say, sometimes. But you will notice that I can also talk a lot with my hands and my arm movements, and with my eyes. I hope you don't mind if I move my hands around and make sounds, but believe it or not, for a lot of people who don't mind it and want to learn, I actually like moving around and using "sign language" and for those who aren't afraid- you can get the feeling to what I'm trying to express. That is- of course- watching and reading my lips. You will be surprised in how quickly we can learn to communicate.

"Aw gee…thanks for the kind words," said Didd as he too moved his hands around in a similar fashion Mute had been using and moved his hand to his heart when he said the word "heart."

"I really like you Mute – and I too felt an instant connection when our eyes first met. And now, I know I've found a friend. I can already understand what you are saying, and I'm sure in the days and months ahead I will learn more and I just love talking to a true kindred soul…and you are indeed a kindred soul," **said Diddley.**

"I'm almost about to cry," said Mute through his green eyes and various hand signals, "Plus- I hope that maybe one day………….one day………….one day…………..you can take a listen to my guitar playing and maybe teach me some things? I like your style and I definitely felt what your playing was saying. Diddley, you are the first person I am telling this to – but way back in the day, this guitar player was starting out way down in Mississippi, and I used to set up for him when he was moving around through the south. Although I was a very young white hillbilly in rags and just begging for any type of work....this great man brought me in and gave me a job setting up as he was trying to start his career. He also saw me holding his guitar one day, and instead of firing me, came over and showed me some chords......he actually let me play his guitar - and secretly gave me some guitar lessons. I practice in secret now when I can find the way."

Diddley almost couldn't speak after hearing/reading Mute's words. Slowly, very slowly, he of asked:

"So Mute.....what was the guitar player's name that was nice to you and gave you those first lessons?

"His name was Robert......he had a different last name when he first started, but then I convinced him to just use his real name.... his full name was Robert Johnson. He went on to become a great musician – a great guitar player – and he was so nice to me when others weren't. I miss Robert so much....haven't heard from him much.

Diddley froze in his seat and couldn't say another word after Mute had told him Robert Johnson was the musician he was talking about. He sat there looking at Mute with his mouth agape. Mute noticed Didd's face, and became alarmed.

"R you Ok Diddley? Did I say something wrong?" said Mute as he waved his arm in front of Diddley's frozen face - no sign language wave- just an everyday, panicked normal wave.

Diddley then snapped out of his frozen maze and replied:

"Oh my goodness – so you knew Robert Johnson?"

"Yes," continued Mute with a faint smile on his face, " as I said – I helped set up his equipment and he was a great gentleman and got me 2 tinkering around on the guitar and the harmonica.

Why do you ask?"

"Mute," said Diddley in shaken words, "I knew Robert Johnson very well from when I was little growing up at grandmother's house in Rundown City, Mississippi. My grandmother Momma Squatt ran the biggest brothel this side of the grand Mississippi, called the Copp-A-Squatt Inn. Just like you and I are new to each other but we see inside each other's souls; Robert was like that to me when I was little and as I grew, he too taught me many things. He showed me the first guitar chords I ever studied - gave me my first guitar lessons as it were – and I'm basically here today because of his encouragement. I will have to one day really explain to you all that he has done for me…. but I'm almost speechless that you knew him and he also taught you some guitar licks. I'd love to hear your guitar playing and can't wait to jam with you. THIS IS SO EXCITING – I JUST CAN'T BELIEVE IT," said Diddley as he let out a:

"WHOOOOOPPPPIIIIEEEEE"

And everybody in the back of the bus woke-up/looked forward at the commotion.

"WHAT IN THE WORLD IS GOING ON!" yelled W.C. from the driver's seat," we got a ways to go you youngins…. don't be "whooopi-e-ing" on W.C's bus - keep it down and let everybody get some sleep. We got about 4/5 hours before we get to Birmingham……. God almighty!"

Mute looked at Diddley and shook him affectionately, with this big smile on his face…. while putting his finger across his lips meaning for Didd not to utter a word….while laughing to himself. He moved close to Diddley's ear and muttered, in a low humorous voice:

"Lil Diddley, we betta calm down and keep this a secret.

Let's talk when we get to our next stop. Don't want to get my boss W.C. riled up. Through it all- I just want to say this is one of the happiest days of my life and I can't wait until we get a chance to sort it all out and I can't wait for you to hear me play some guitar and blow my harmonica....so I say WHOOOPPPPIEE TOO!"

"I agree," whispered Diddley, *"can't wait to talk to you again......let's get some sleep."*

CHAPTER 6
MUTE, RACISM, AND WELCOME TO BIRMINGHAM

Diddley dosed off for an hour or two. He woke after a couple of hour's naps and gazed out his window- one of his favorite pastimes instead of sleeping. It was near evening – he figured they'd be in Birmingham soon. The state of Alabama was actually beautiful from a country standpoint – green trees everywhere……. and farms…..and trees….. and farms. Somebody had mentioned that Alabama was known for not just its farming and cotton fields, but was a huge provider in lumber for the rest of the United States. Diddley could see why – miles and miles of pine and other trees; with workers, both black and white – although mainly the blacks were manual workers while the whites were supervising - cutting down trees on various types of lands and hauling/logging it here and there. In one instance, as the Betty Boop Chitlin Hilton was slowly going around this curved part of town – I think W.C. d mentioned to those up front that they were passing through a city called Jackson, Alabama, Diddley saw these four young black workers – maybe no older them him – at the helm of this wagon being pulled by two mules. The wagon had some chains hooked to the back, and the chains were wrapped around these massive hulks of pine trees that had been cut and splintered and ready for hauling. The wagon was heading right around the same path as the Betty Boop, and since the bus was moving so slowly, Diddley opened up the window, stuck his neck out, and was able to get the four black youngster's attention holding the reins on the mules.

"Hey young brothers- how you doing!" Diddley yelled.

"We doing just fine!" the four guys yelled back by taking off their hats and whooping and yelling.

"We are heading to Birmingham…. I play on the Chitlin Circuit," yelled Didd as he continued to wave his hands.

"You are one lucky young stud," said the guy holding the reins, "We are from this small city called Thomasville, but we all catch the bus each morning to work in Jackson cause that's where the work is. Please have fun playing ya music. We've seen the Betty B pass by here many times, and my brothers and I have layed awake many nights just wishing that one day we could do something and see other parts of this country. You are the first person to actually talk to us from the bus – thank ya."

"I hope you know how lucky you are young buck," said one of the other brothers in the seat holding the reins," to be in a bus seat on an adventure to another city and not on this dad-blastit wagon hauling this dad-blastit wood."

"Hang on my friends……. if you have dreams to do other things- never give up those dreams!" yelled Diddley out the window as he looked ahead and could tell the bus road would soon clear straight and break away from the road of the young brothers.

"Thank you, our new friend……. we've tried to get the attention of others on the Bett B before, but I guess they didn't want to talk – you are the first. Thank you for talking to us," they said as the road began to curve and they would soon go their separate ways. "Good luck in ya career….and maybe one day we can make it to the big city and see you perform. You keep your dreams alive also…………. My name is Eugene Thompson and these are my cousin's Lil Bud, Frank, and Cutter - WHAT'S YOUR NAME?" was the last thing Didd heard as the bus would soon be under a tunnel.

"I'M DIDDLEY SQUATT – HOPE TO SEE YOU BROTHERS ONE DAY AGAIN!" said Diddley as they all waved goodbye to each other as the bus was about to enter a tunnel. However, just before the bus entered the tunnel and leave all the fields and the workers – W.C. shouted from the front of the bus:

"NOT THERE YET - AND NO CITY AREAS AROUND ANYPLACE CLOSE. SO………WE GONNA STOP FOR AWHILE AND LET ANYBODY WHO NEEDS TO HANDLE THEIR BUSINESS- YOU KNOW WHAT I MEAN……. HANDLE THEIR

BUSINESS - OR MAYBE TAKE A QUICK STRETCH AND SHORT WALK - BUT IT WON'T BE A LONG BREAK. GEESH!"

The Betty Boop then pulled over to the side of the road....and Diddley looked behind and could see the black folks he had thought he just waved goodbye to - were running to the bus. But it wasn't just Eugene Thompson and Lil Bud, and the guys behind the horses – BUT NOW HE COULD SEE FOLKS RUNNING TOWARD THE BUS WHO HAD BEEN IN THE FIELDS PICKING VARIOUS VEGETABLES AND CORN OR COTTON OR WHATEVER?

Somebody on the bus said:

"They just excited that for maybe the first time the Betty Boop is stopping......they just curious to see some other black folks dressed other than in work clothes. Let's be nice and talk to them."

"Shit....I ain't talking to no damn field workers...........y'all crazy," said Treach as other performers headed to the front to exit and greet the field workers.

"Don't listen to Treach," Stan said to Diddley as he passed by, "we can make these folks day....... let's go meet these hard working folks!'

Everybody exited the bus except Treach....... even Tessa made it off the bus without Treach knowing.

As the performers were standing along the side of the bus, Dorothea, as one of the elder statespersons on the tour, spoke out loud from the side of the bus:

"We are the performers on the current Chitlin Circuit Tour. We are blessed to finally stop and meet all you hard working, beautiful people who we have passed – and waved at - for soooo many years. It is our honor to stop and greet you. We do not have much time, but we will share our names first, and could you all just yell your names afterward........we love to hear the real names of people."

'YEAH!" the workers screamed out.

The Chitlin Circuit performers, as well as all the helpers, went down the line and said their names.

Then – the workers who made it to the bus started YELLING their names:

One group of men: "I'm Kelvin, Anthony here, I'm Dennis, Lance here, Eli, John, Herbert, Herman, Reggie, Arthur, Paul, Britches, Doug, Mike, Mario, William, Jaco, Chauncey, Patches, Wendell, Arthur, Gordon, Skip, Fred, Othel, Genaro, Steve, Thomas, Kevin, Fulton, David, Justus, James, Terrance, Michael, Ronald, Tito, AJ, Gio, Marcus, Bemo, Skip, Maxcy, Darryl, Gary, Kyle."

A group of women: "I'm Janice, hello...Arinn here, I'm Faviola, Tita, Maxine, Stephanie, Tania, Norena, Deanna, Lauren, Sherry, Jean, Deborah, Duane, Donna, Tracy, Della, Sylvia, Saundra, Rochelle, Erica, Floyda, Blondell, Teresa, Pam, Elaine, Rhonda, Rochelle, Regina, Deborah, Dianna, Barbara Jean, Beatrice, Marsha, Elaine."

The performers and workers then ran together and hugged and shook hands, laughed......some went behind the trees and did indeed "handle their business." IT WAS SOMETHING.

"OK......... WE GOTTA GO!" came W.C's voice.

Everybody said their goodbyes. Some laughed, some wept....

Everybody was soon back on the Betty Boop after the short break and various conversations. The bus soon chucked along as it entered into the tunnel. Diddley found his seat, closed the window gently, and sat back in his seat. He just loved meeting everyday people.

"Everyday People?" said Diddley," maybe one day that will be a song title," He took out his journal and wrote down the words "Everyday People" for a song title..........and then Sly woke up and poked his head out of his poach.

"Did somebody say "Everyday People?" I really like the sound of that," said Sly before grabbing a couple of nuts and heading back into the inner depths of his home. "See - I'm Everyday People and I also like to Stand and tell my fellow peeps and animals that You Can Make It If You Try!"

The bus drove on and Diddley drifted off-and-on back to sleep.... however, he still had his new Alabama tree haulers, filed, folks, and all he just met - in his thoughts.

"WAKE UP EVERYBODY - WELCOME TO BIRMINGHAM"

Diddley's eyes opened from the unmistakable word's W.C. just yelled. - that was definitely W.C. and if he wanted to get your attention!

"We are now entering the grand city of Birmingham, Alabama, and all of its rich ness and deep-south culture. Birmingham is the *real* south, so I always need to say something before my passengers depart the Betty B. Now....as your unofficial tour guide, I know a bunch of you folks have been on this tour and already know about Birmingham and certain rules about town that you must obey, but I just want to pass along to any newbies....and I think by you "newbies" ya'll know who I'm talking about (hey hey) - to just be mindful of who you are talking to and what establishments to visit and some of the rules. If you have any questions, talk to some of your fellow musician friends and they will school you on what's going on down here in Birmingham and other cities in the South. I think you know that old W.C. here is your friend, and I don't agree at all with how some of these white folks see the world- but – it is what it is right now in the world. I just want everyone to be safe and I do appreciate y'all and all the great service and music you provide out into the world. So please, be careful."

Diddley continued looking out the window at the busy city, as the folks walked along the downtown bustling crowded, yet peaceful, streets, some impeccable dressed with their ladies around their arms......school kids holding books and looking in the windows at candy shops; while others wore overalls and work clothes from working in the fields.

W.C came on the speaker again:

"We are pulling up to a hotel next to the world-famous Carver Theater. Everybody, please take your time getting off the bus and the helpers will help you check in and get to your rooms with your luggage. Old W.C is sure you folks will slay that Carver audience tomorrow and we will then move onto our next stop. Be safe now.....you hear."

The bus pulled into the "One Night Stand Motel" which was adjacent to the Carver Theater. As Diddley looked out the window, he could see the folks walking around the bustling downtown Birmingham downtown area and once again he got excited at seeing city life unfold- although it was now moving into the night.

Since Diddley was in the front, he was one of the first persons to get off the bus. He hopped down, and proceeded to help all the performers off the bus. Most of them were very gracious and gave Diddley a "thank you young man" as he helped them step down.... although the last of the performers (of course Treach) gave him a strange look and refused his help -Diddley felt not out of meanness, but maybe just because he was the newbie and that was like some sort of initiation to the Chitlin Circuit? Diddley didn't care at this point, he was just excited to be in a newer bigger city and this would be his second chance to showcase his skills to an audience that never heard of him.

W.C. hit the ground and his words were the next:

"Ladies and Gentlemen – you have a free night tonight. You are on your own after you check into your rooms – but please, remember WHERE we are and WHO you are, and obey all rules. Tomorrow we will be ready to entertain the folks of Birmingham, and then it's on to Atlanta, Georgia. Folks, be safe tonight and I'll see everybody' tomorrow."

Diddley checked into his room, his gig bag slung over his shoulder, and Mute helped him with his lone duffle bag of clothes where Diddley kept all his other worldly possessions. After Mute dropped the bag into the room, he mouthed the words:

"Maybe we can get together later for dinner and get to know each other a little more. Take some time to get settled and I be back. Slappy Fox and King D.D., de are my best friends on the tour – maybe they can join us."

"Sounds good to me," Diddley told Mute and slapped him on the shoulder as Mute headed out the door.

"Ok Sly…..it's just you and me my best friend…..come on out and let's catch up and shoot the breeze cool breeze," said Diddley.

"I'm already out, you waaaay behind the great Sly's mind!" came Sly's voice as he was indeed already out of his pouch home and chewing a nut while looking out the room window, "you ain't gotta tell me when it's time to escape……..this is Sly you talking to after all."

"So far, so good somewhat on the tour," said Didd," I hope you are enjoying the experience as much as me. While the music is important, I'm also enjoying meeting different people and I especially like looking out of the bus window and seeing the different sights. I like the mountains and the valleys the most….just God's gifts of nature; but, I also enjoy when we pass through the towns and seeing the people going about their day to day lives. I like to look at their faces and expressions to see if they are enjoying this strange thing called life....it's looking in their eyes and their expressions that intrigue a new song out of me. I'm just happy where I'm at right now."

"Diddley – you are indeed one strange guy? Looking at strange people's faces? And passing a valley with some trees?.....and maybe listening to some cows "moooo" and some mules "he-haw?" That's what gets you off really after being booed? You didn't even mention maybe seeing the girls in the skimpy dresses? Now...I know you like girls- I'm not going in the other direction – it's just weird the stuff that excites you. Please don't mention this to these folks on the tour bus – they will think you are the weirdest human being ever," said Sly as he flew across the room and fell on the bed while crossing his paws across his stomach with laughter.

"Everybody is different my "animal" friend, may I remind you," said Diddley while also chuckling," might I remind you how different our relationship is? Just remember how many human friends you have talked to in your lifetime and they've also talked back," Diddley fell on the bed next to Sly with them both holding their stomachs in laughter.

While lying on their backs, both looking up at the ceiling, they began a quick dialogue:

"So, who do like or most relate to on the tour thus far?" asked Sly.

"Good question," said Diddley," I really feel for Tessa Treu and what I suspect she must be living with. I hope it can eventually be worked out, because she can really sing and seems like a truthful person. I really, really respect the elders of the group – Dorethea and Sam Bluester and – I watch and listen to their every word when they sing or talk directly to me.....it's like Momma Squatt and the ladies at the Copp-A-Squatt giving me the elderly advice I need and miss. I've always respected my elders, because they have been there before me and it would be crazy to not listen to their advice and comments.

"OK" was all Sly could muster.

"I also like and respect Slappy Fox. Slappy is sooo funny and he makes me laugh and move on from some of the tragic things that are happening in this world, and with me personally. He told me that "laughter" makes the world better and is the best medicine when you are feeling depressed or alone – so when he tells me a joke or says something even funny about my name – it makes me laugh. King D.D.? I respect him so much because like me, he is a guitarist. He gave me positive feedback from the gate, so I will always respect him and listen to any criticism, suggestions, or comments- to improve my craft.

"I like them all my brother," said Sly as he groped upward onto Diddley's chest, "but I got a feeling there is one more person you like," said Sly as picked at a piece of popcorn.

"You know me better than anybody you Sly dog! Of course, I'm thrilled most with meeting Mute and learning how to communicate with him. We just bonded immediately, probably because I can understand what he must have gone through in his life to this point. I was bullied growing up just because of a funny name; can you imagine what Mute must have gone through because of not being able to talk and communicate? But he kept going......"

Sly laughed.

"Actually – I was thinking you liked Tessa best because she is fine as wine. Maybe Mute second?"

"Funny!" chimed in Diddley, "But Mute is more like me............ I'm going through some new stuff and adventures and he saw that right away and has offered to help in any way he can. I like that! Although I haven't done it a lot yet. I think I will like reaching back and helping those in similar situations – nothing makes you feel better in life……..not fame…..not money……..not nuts (chuckle)…..just reaching back and offering to help. It's like "paying it forward," – somebody helped you – so you should help somebody in return and not expect any monetary or other worldly reward in return. It just makes you feel better period!"

"If you say so my brother," said Sly while searching Diddley dead in his eyes, "but a beautiful woman is hard to beat. I sometimes think about this guy God you talk about, that you read about from the Bible thingy, and which your grandma and others preached to you about – he was and is one powerful cat because when I've been with you and thought it was all gonna fall apart – you continue to just push through and make it through to the other side. Unbelievable……..I can just tell that you are never going to give up and pursue your dreams wherever they take you. I've never met a person, or an animal, with what you got."

Didd couldn't believe it – but he thought he saw a tear fall from Sly's eye?

"Is that a tear falling from your eye?" asked Diddley

"NO – THAT'S NOT A TEAR," said Sly shyly as he left Didd's stomach and skirted once again to the window sill, "I got a piece of this goddarn popcorn stuck in my eye…..Squirrel's chew hard you know."

Diddley reached over and petted Sly on the back.

"You'll always be my number one friend, till death!" said Diddley.

"I hope so, "said Sly, "and we still got a whole lot of living to do so remember that. Let's get some sleep before one of your human friends knocks on the door……..yeah…I heard that Mute guy saying he wanted to go out to dinner with you and a few of his friends. Remember, I hear everything."

"Sleep it is," said Diddley.

The two spread out on the bed and took a nice peaceful, nap after the long bus ride.

Later that night indeed came a knock on the door. Sly awoke and found a hiding place when Diddley moved to the door.

"Wake up young breeze. Whatcha doing napping with your young self," came the voice of Slappy Fox. With him was King D.D. and Mute.

"We thought we'd take you out to dinner and show you some of Birmingham since you are the newbie to the tour," said Slappy, "See…..as a tradition, some of the older cats have the responsibility to show the new performers on the tour/to kind of help mentor them along the way, what they call "the ropes of the tour." Some of the performers don't do it, but King D.D. and I have always believed in helping out. We saw you talking to young Mute earlier and thought it would be OK to bring somebody your age along. So, Mr. Young Diddley, grab your coat and let's go grab some grub. I don't know about anybody else, but I'm so hungry I could eat a horse and then chase the rider and have him for dessert!

"Sounds good to me," Diddley said as he grabbed his coat and they were out the door.

As they walked down the infamous Fourth Avenue next to 7th Street North, Diddley couldn't help but feel the electricity in the air. The streets were bustling with both black and white (mainly) folks walking in pretty good clothes – since it was a happening night – and the ladies were all dressed up in dresses and hats and heels. As they passed the few black people, Diddley's group and the folks on the street said "hey – how you doing brothers" and slapped 5's and it was like family. Nothing from the white folks though.

Slappy said "You know what – let's take youngblood to another part of town, I hear they have some different type of food at this new restaurant."

"Fine with me," said King D.D., "Slappy – let's just get some place and eat. You the jokester, you ever heard the joke I'm so hungry I could eat my elbows" they all laughed as a cab pulled up and they jumped into the back.

"Zooooooooooooooooooooooooooooooooooooooooooo ooooooooooooooom."

Soon they were in a different part of Birmingham......the buildings were not as stately....more country looking........and most of the folks walking by were of a prominently different hue.....definitely more white. That quickly, and they were in a different section of Birmingham.

"You.... you sure this is good idea?" said King D.D. with an uneasy look in his eyes.

"Yeah – we just going for a quick bite...this white comic friend of mine told me this place makes as good a fried chicken as our momma's......and I want's me some good fried chicken," Slappy said with a laugh.

The cab pulled up to a restaurant with the title "HTBH&C - Ham Towns Best Ham and Chicken" in bright blinking lights above the restaurant. There were some locals -all white- hanging out in the front of the store – some sitting on barrels or rickety wooden stools; others sitting on the tailgates of their trucks or leaning on the back of their cars. Most were smoking cigarettes, and they were passing around various bottles of alcohol. Didd and his friends exited the cab right out front of everybody. Right away, Diddley could feel these locals eying his group very suspiciously. The others must have felt the same, because King D.D.'s first words were "Slappy...what have you got us into?"

"We just gonna order something quickly and go...no big deal," said Slappy. Diddley looked at Mute, and he could tell even he was a bit suspect about where they were. As they moved to the door, Diddley saw a sign that read:

"NO COLOREDS ALLOWED TO SIT INSIDE - YOU CAN ORDER TO GO THOUGH."

"Slappy…. what have you done?' said King D.D.

"My bad…….MY friend never mentioned this place was off limits to black folks?…just wait till I meet him again – if ever – I'mma talk his white ass black!. Let me at least try to go in and order us some chicken dinners and we will be outta here."

"You not gonna leave us out here alone," said King D.D. as all four of them cautiously went through the front door. There was a counter to the left with maybe 12 seats – 6 of them open. So, if things were fair and good in this crazy world - the four of them could have sat as they ordered and waited for the food to be fixed. However, all of them stayed huddled together and moved in unison to the side of the cash register where a sign read "ORDER HERE TO GO." As they inched forward, Diddley's eyes were wide open observing the customer's faces. For some reason, Diddley, unlike the others, was more curious than afraid???…………he was always curious to experience situations he had only heard about…..and this would appear to be one of those times in his young life. The girls at the Copp-A-Squatt had warned him that he might have encounters such as this- and to just stay calm and let the others speak. He was warned some white folks weren't too thrilled with black folks coming to their towns……….so Diddley was strangely excited………. It was like he was taking photos with his eyes and transferring them to his brain with each step - as they moved forward – and for some reason he was excited.

The customers inside were definitely not happy to see 3 black men with a white guy in their restaurant. They looked at each one – eyeing them first from their heads and faces – and then their eyes drifted down to the shoes each of them were wearing. There were more than just stares and murmurs, Didd heard comments like:

"What the hell? Better hurry up and bring me my order – I don't like this place serving niggers" and,

"Can't we a have a place of our own?. What the hell is happening to this world;" to,

"I understand all businesses need to make money, but you don't see me in the black niggertown section of Birmingham ordering my chicken?"

This old fat white lady with thick glasses, white hair, apron, a cigarette dangling from the side of her wrinkled lips- and a pencil behind her ear, was sitting behind the counter ready to quickly take the intruders order.

"What y'all want to order, let's hurry up. We only doing this because of all these new laws trying to sweep this country, and ending this Jim Crow whatever the hell that is - talking about trying to make food establishments and nigras equal – and lord knows I need business. Who the hell is Jim Crow anyway and what the hell has he got to be crowing about? I'll take your orders and get you some food – but you damn sure can't sit here and eat it. Now – quickly, what y'all want so you can move on back to where you come from."

Slappy spoke for the group.

"Yes ma'am……. we are traveling musicians and just got into town. My name is Slappy Fox and I'm a comedian…this here is the world-famous blues guitarist King D.D.; next to him is an up and coming artist I'm sure all the world will hear about one day by the name of Diddley Squatt – and this white friend of ours is called Mute……he sets up all our equipment."

"WE AIN'T THE FBI? YOU AIN'T REGISTERING FOR THE ARMY IS YOU? SHE DIDN'T ASK YOU FOR ALL YOUR NAMES?' came the voice of one of the regulars sitting at the counter who stood up after hearing Slappy talk. This guy was really upset....... had on a straw hat with the confederate flag draped across the front; had on overalls and a dirty white t-shirt – and a piece of straw in the corner of his mouth.

The rest of the regulars broke out into guffaws , snickers, and laughter.

As Diddley and his crew saw the men laughing.....they guessed maybe they better laugh also. So they chuckled for safety reasons........but not loud chuckles.

"By the way," said the confederate-flag-overall guy, "did you say one of your names was Diddley Squatt? Really.....what kind of a name is Diddley Squatt for a nigger?"

This elicited a rousing, second round of laughter from the Ham Town regulars. One of the older guys almost fell off his stool he was bending over laughing so hard!

"Yes...you got that right" said Slappy with his muted chuckle, "you for sure will one day hear the music of Mr. Diddley Squatt and he will be famous....and you know what y'all can say...you can say that the reason that made him famous because one day he came to town and ate at the world famous Ham Towns Best Ham and Chicken," said Slappy as he slapped his thigh and the regulars erupted info further laughter.

"Now," said Slappy as the laughter started to die down, "let us have 4 ham sandwiches, 4 sides of collard greens, and 12 pieces of your friend chicken – and of course – THAT IS OF COURSE TO GO!"

--------------MORE LAUGHTER------------

The waitress lady stopped laughing long enough to take down the order, turn toward the kitchen area where the food was cooked, and yell out the order and ended it with, "and be sure to say this order is for Diddley Squatt!"

--------------MORE LAUGHTER--------------

"Thank you ma'am, " said Diddley as he stuck out his hand in hopes of shaking the waitress's hand.........he also had .5 cents he was going to offer her as a tip.

"I DON'T SHAKE NO NIGGER'S HAND – YOU FOOL. MY HUSBAND WOULD KILL ME. AND .5 CENTS FOR A TIP? I CAN SEE WHY YOUR NAME IS DIDDLEY SQUATT – CUZ YOU DEFINITELY DON'T KNOW SQUATT!" said the waitress as she waved a napkin at Diddley.....and said to the others:

"OK.....y'all can move back outside and wait....and I'll bring you your order when it is ready," she wiped tears of laughter and mild anger from her eyes with the napkin.

The four moved back outside and were laughing........ actually more for the benefit and safety of themselves – than actually laughing with the regulars- and the obvious racism – from the regulars.....they eyed Diddley a little suspiciously for offering to shake hands. Diddley had heard that for black folks, from his many mentors, that when you are in a perilous and unknown situation, it is best to just play along with certain white folk and not jeopardize the situation with your true feelings. Better to be safe than sorry.

As the four waited outside, King D.D., Slappy, and Mute all lit up cigarettes. I guess they felt no need to discuss Diddley's attempt at being nice. Diddley saw a tree with nuts on the ground next to the restaurant, so he ran over quickly and started throwing nuts in his pocket – something for his good buddy Sly. Mute took out his Pal-Mal cigarette box and ran over offered it to Didd.

"No thanks Mute....I don't smoke man, " Diddley mouthed back at Mute. "Luckily, cigarettes don't do anything for me. Kind of like alcohol.....I just don't need it man."

Mute mouthed back with a smile:

"Wha? U don smoke or drink anything?"

"Never had a drink," said Diddley, "believe me…growing up at the Copp-A-Squatt Inn in Mississippi, I saw first-hand the effects of alcohol and what it made people do. I saw very few people who I would say could handle alcohol and still progress in their lives……I'm sure it is possible…..but I never saw it. I tasted alcohol once, and I spat it out….so nothing for me."

"That good," said Mute, " I like how you think for yourself……..you will listen to others- but in da end you are you!"

"What's that ya'll talking about," said Slappy as he ambled over, "you and Mute seem to have a special relationship."

"Yeah," chimed in King D.D., "I been on this Chitlin Circuit route many times with Mute, but he seem to like you more than anybody else I've known about."

"I don't know," said Diddley," I just seem to really like and appreciate people who are shortchanged in life, through no fault of their own – but they learn how to get through life and to become productive in something. I just really gravitate toward people like Mute….it is like mystical….but I love it and I look forward to always looking for different people and how they handle their shortcomings. These folks are really my heroes as much as Robert Johnson, and both you Kind D.D. and Slappy….it is just something that God put in me and I love it!"

"Yeah," said King D.D., "Slappy and I were both saying how your ears and eyes open with curiosity when something possibly confrontational may be about to happen….and instead of getting upset, you listen and seem calm. Just like now when we were ordering our food. Must say, I've never met a young black boy with such calmness."

"Just being me," said Diddley," just being me. I prefer peace and listening over yelling and fighting…..and I hope to project this in some of my songs. I think the world could use it."

Their take-out order soon arrived, so coincidentally at the same time as their taxi-cab – and wouldn't you know WHO would bring the order ?? – none other than confederate-flag- overall guy.

"Here's ya'lls order....I want to give it to the Diddley Squatt guy,"' he said with the bag of food in his outstretched left-hand.

"Didd.... get!' motioned Slappy for Diddley to grab the bag.

As Diddley reached for the bag, the confederate-flag-overrall guy REACHED HIS RIGHT ARM BACK AND THREW HIS BALLED FIST DIRECTLY INTO DIDDLEY'S RIGHT EYE- A PUNCH UNLIKE DIDDLEY HAD EVER RECEIVED. DIDDLEY FLOPPED TO THE GROUND IN BOTH SURPISE AND PAIN.

"DON'T YOU EVER FLIRT, DISRESPECT, OR TRY TO ACT NICE TO MY WIFE OR ANY OTHER WHITE WOMAN – YOU GOT THAT MR. DIDDLEY SQUATT!" screamed the confederate-flag-overall guy.

King D.D., Slappy, and Mute shot over and hovered over Diddley.

"You OK?" they all asked.

"What happened? Why did he do that?" said Diddley as he grabbed his eye and winced in pain as it started to swell. They helped him to his feet.

"So ya'll get on now – that was just a warning. I know this black fool is a youngin – but let that be a warning experience......now get in that taxi cab and get back to your part of town!' said confederate-flag-overall guy.

Mute and the others looked over to the restaurant and could

see the other regulars looking their way, and they knew without question their best option was to get in the taxi-cab as soon as possible and skedaddle.

They helped Diddley to the cab and SWOOSHHHHH....were soon on their way on the highway – and Slappy indeed held the food bag.

SILENCE IN THE CAB..............THEN:

"Learning experience," said King D.D, "glad you didn't try to fight back.....it wasn't the time or place.....you are definitely a mystical cat and handle stuff differently."

"Wasn't your fault at all youngblood," said Slappy," you were just trying to be nice. I guess he thought he had to try and protect his women in front of his friends.......although I saw him reach down and pick up the nickel as we left."

"Not yer falt," slathered Mute," some white people just are mean and don't like different. I'm sorry white people don't like black guys saying anything to white women....one day it will change......but Emmitt Till- I don't know what to say."

Diddley, holding the napkin on his eye, finally said " Well......I will be very careful in the future when talking to white women and others.......I will just sit back and let others do the talking and I'll just watch. I guess you do learn from your mistakes – even if you don't think you made a mistake. I'm just glad we got out of there safely."

After the punch, Mute, King D.D., Slappy, and Diddley were soon back to the One Night Stand Motel. In the lobby, Diddley took out his journal and jotted down some of what he had just experienced; especially the fight and stuff King D.D., Slappy, and Mute had told him about how he seemed mystical and to handle stuff differently. Maybe some of their words would make a good song one day.

Slappy opened the restaurant container and split the food evenly between the four. It certainly looked and smelled delicious! Everyone said goodnight, and then split to their respective rooms. When Diddley entered his room and put the food on the table, Sly came from behind him and jumped on his shoulder as a surprise.

"GOTCHA!" he said as he flew in front of Diddley's face with this wide grin on his squirrely face.

'WHAT IN THE FREAKING WORLD HAPPENED TO YOUR EYE!' said Sly as he got right in Diddley's face examining every inch of his skin.

"Just another road life, learning lesson," said Diddley – he even laughed a bit.

"That must've been some lesson!" said Sly, "you wanna spill all the details?"

"Not tonight.... I'm exhausted," said Diddley, "maybe another time down the road. Tonight, were nuts. The good thing is I didn't forget my best friend."

"Speaking of nuts?" slurred Sly.

Diddley reached into his pocket and threw fresh nuts all over the table.

"Of course, I didn't forget about my buddy."

Sly flew back and forth across the room, dancing on the table tops, the night stands, the bed, the dresser – just everywhere – ecstatic that he had some fresh nuts.

"How lucky is this Mr. Sly Squinter Squirrel to have a friend like Diddley Squatt? I must be the luckiest squirrel in the world....and we get to go on all these adventures." Once again

Diddley thought he saw a tear fall from Sly's eyes.

"Enjoy my friend……..now let's eat and be thankful for our meal. Tomorrow is a big show at the Carver Theater – and we need to impress. I think I will try out some of my new songs. So eat and be merry!"

Diddley tore into the chicken…..Sly likewise his nuts.

CHAPTER 7
CONCERT NIGHT AT THE CARVER THEATRE

Concert night. Carver Theater, Birmingham, Alabama. In the back-dressing rooms.

Diddley is nervous. Having only played a couple of performances, and of course – the most recent majority negative response to his performance at the Harlem Duke.

But tonight, is the night he has decided to do something different – regardless of what others have suggested because of his last negative response ......he is still going to try something new and different. He has decided to first talk/rap, and then to sing to the world his first really original song. What the hell – he is Diddley Squatt right? Let it flow!

Didd will be the next-to-last act tonight, actually the last act before the always headliners Treach and Tessa Treu Revue, come on to close the show - and the crowd is anxious to hear the headliners. That's okay – Didd doesn't care, JUST LET IT FLOW AND HAPPEN.

All the other acts have played – with only Diddley and the closers left.

Didd walks out.......and with the spotlight on him.... speaks confidently into the microphone

"Thank you, Carver Theater patrons, - to those willing to listen to my set. Yes.... I'm the new talent. And I want to tell you – I'm not afraid. I've had my ups and downs, so has everyone – correct? So, I'm just gonna let it fly tonight – respond as you like. I want to sing to you my first original song and I hope you like it. I'm going to talk and rap a little first – then sing. You have your right to your opinion...but I'm just going to go for it!"

The house blues band begins a very, very slow hum of music.... kind of a basic blues roundup that they would play for any musician first entering the stage. Very mellow and calm.

Slow...
slow...slow........................

Diddley in the front of the stage at the microphone:

"So, this is it! My name is Diddley Squatt. That's my real name. I am blessed to be at the Carver Theatre – and will give you my best. Just a quick bit about me and my music. I'm sure you can imagine with the name of Diddley Squatt I have been teased and ridiculed my entire life. I get it. However, I do not let the ridicules and comments bother me..........I learned to deal with the name calling long ago with help from my mentors and friends – both human and animal friends- so my skin is thick as a brick and that doesn't bother me anymore. I'm more concerned with presenting feel good music and songs to the world that might help you get through your hardship – whatever it might be – and get you from Monday through Sunday!

(they crowd cheers......." YEAH")

I am proud to say my grandmother Momma-Squatt is the owner and proprietor of the Copp-A Squatt-Inn in Rundown, Mississippi."

"So enough of the talk for now – that's all I have to say.... but I still gotta sing! I hope you enjoy this song I recently wrote. It's called *"Moments That Take Your Breath Away."* It may start off slow and easy – but wait until the end! Hope you like my song:"

A slow.......... mellow groove.... emanates from Diddley's guitar and the background musicians follow suit.... bass, organ, horns.......

"Moments That Take Your Breath Away"

(chorus/refrain)

Diddley sings:

"Moments that take your breath away

Are the memories that keep you strong

Just remember at the end of the day

That your rights outweigh your wrongs"

So, I'm a young cat, but I listen to those who are older

And I like to write whatever I hear

And you can bet I listen, and then I write it in my folder

See, I love music because of my ear and the mentors I've met

This here guitar, once belonged to a famous Robert cat

Robert Johnson was a mentor, sat aside in many of his sets

People listen, and remember to push peace and love

Because not one of us is a perfect person

Except the guy in the sky, I'm talking our Lord above

(chorus/refrain)

The background singers sing:

"Moments that take your breath away

Are the memories that keep you strong

Just remember at the end of the day

That your rights outweigh your wrongs"

Diddley singing again:

"I know my name is different; I hope you read my inner thoughts

Everything in life is different, and has to progress

But if you haven't stood for your principles,

then you haven't fought the fought

Life is unpredictable, and life is strange but true

You can't spend your time trying to satisfy others

You gotta keep pushing and never give up

You can't be nobody but the real you

(chorus/refrain)

"Moments that take your breath away

Are the memories that keep you strong

Just remember at the end of the day

That your rights outweigh your wrongs"

Diddley singing again:

"You can't be anybody-other than the real you

If you think I'm lying – turn your black to blue

But if you think I'm right, then stand and shout out

Because you are you – and that's what it' s all it's about

So, stand people, and sing this refrain for long

Because, your rights outweigh your wrongs!

Diddley then unwraps the guitar from his shoulder, places it on his guitar stand, and moves to center stage. He then grabs the microphone as the crowd is building into a frenzy, undoubtedly thinking "what is this youngblood about to do?"

Diddley: "When I say rights, you say wrongs!"

Diddley: "RIGHTS"

Crowd: "WRONGS"

Diddley: "RIGHTS"

Crowd: "WRONGS"

Diddley: "Now wave your hands in the air………………and let's sing it again like you just don't care! Ya'll ready……here we go!"

THE CROWD IS NOW IN A FRENZY AND THEY HAVE GOTTEN OUT OF THEIR CHAIRS; WAVING THEIR ARMS - AND STANDING IN FRONT OF THE STAGE!!!!!!

Diddley: "RIGHTS"

Crowd: "WRONGS"

Diddley: "RIGHTS"

Crowd: "WRONGS"

Diddley then raises his arms………..and to the surprise of everyone…. dives into the audience…..who miraculously catch him with their extended arms raised……and with their hands, start moving him overhead from one side of the theater to the next….while Diddley acts like he is swimming through the small crowd. After a while, Diddley points toward the stage and the crowd pushes him to the stage. Diddley gets back on stage, and throws his guitar strap back around his neck. He then says "ONE LAST TIME!"

Diddley: "RIGHTS"

Crowd: "WRONGS"

Diddley: "RIGHTS"

Crowd: "WRONGS

Diddley then calms down….and the crowd senses the same….and it appears they are on Diddley's wavelength and just waiting and willing do whatever Diddley says.

Diddley moves to the reconstructed microphone where it first began………and sings the last refrain:

"So that's my story, and I'm sticking to it till the end

I hope you listened and listened to what I had to say

And just always remember – Diddly Squatt is your friend!"

(chorus/refrain)

Chorus:

"Moments that take your breath away

Are the memories that keep you strong

Just remember at the end of the day

That your rights outweigh your wrongs"

Twang…. twang……and the drummer hits the last beat. Diddley falls to his knees in front of the crowd:

and

and

and

THE CROWD GOES CRAZY! THEY ARE STANDING AND CLAPPING……THEY HAVE NO IDEA WHAT THEY HAVE JUST SEEN…BUT THEY KNOW IT WAS DIFFERENT!

Diddley moves to the side of the stage……..hoisting his guitar in his right hand above his head….as the crowd continues to yell and scream. The house band behind him is in disbelief…they had never seen an ending like Diddley had just presented……jumping into the crowd and not falling?

As Diddley exits stage left, the first person that greets him is Mute with a towel in his hand. He wipes Diddley's sweating face and gives him a hug at the same time.

He then pushes Diddley back, looks him in the eyes, and starts this exhilarating hand-signing craziness……..obviously excited about what he just witnessed. His hands are flaring all up-and-down/criss-crossing….flaying all over because he is so excited. He then points to Diddley and looks deep and dead into his eyes. Diddley stops and watches Mutes mouth – he knows Mute has something important to express.

"DAT WAS FANTASTIC" says Mute through broken language, "WHAT A BOUNCE BACK – YOU DID IT DIDDLEY – OVERCAME YOUR FIRST FAILURE AND MOVED ON…. UNBELIVABLE. DIDDLY>>>>>>>DID<<<<<DID>>>>>> CONTINUE TO ALWAYS BE YOURSELF AND PLAY WHAT YO WANT TO PLAY….BE YOURSLEF ONSTAGE….YOU ARE GOING TO MAKE A CHANGE!" as Mute hugs him again and continues to dry him off with his towel.

"Thanks Mute…. I appreciate your words my brother!" Didd says sincerely directly back into Mute's eyes, making sure to mouth each word slowly so Mute understands. Mute obviously does – because a big grin then encompasses his face. As Diddley moves through the hallway behind the stage many of the performers stop to issue a word with Diddley. Slappy Fox and Jack Leg Batey are ecstatic! "That was GREAT" shouts Jack Leg Batey, "little brother, you just continue to be you!"

"You trying to shock these folks to death! Can't wait to see you before a larger crowd" laughs Slappy Fox as he slaps Diddley on the back. "The young lady next to me was having such a fine time during your guitar solo…. I swear……she took off her underwear and was about to throw it on stage……..cept it was so big….it didn't make it to the stage!"

Next came King D.D.:

"That was definitely different young Diddley," said King as he graciously and truthfully took Didd's hand and squeezed it, "You didn't let that last show response bother you. While I must definitely say it was something different.... but who am I to say something different and new might be good or even fruitful. The world needs new."

Stan the Lizard Man? While Didd was talking to someone else, Stan crept up behind Diddley and put one of his pet lizards on Diddley's shoulder. While most people would have maybe screamed and yelled and cursed.........Diddley simply looked over at the lizard and smiled.....Diddley reached up and grabbed and said to the lizard.

"Hey buddy.... did you dig Diddley's performance?"

THOSE AROUND BURST INTO LAUGHTER....... they all couldn't believe Diddley's calmness at finding a lizard on one's shoulder and not freaking out. Diddley stroked the lizard's underbelly as he turned and found Stan.

"You are definitely a different human being, "said Stan laughing as he took the lizard and continued to laugh, "most people would have freaked out and I would probably be kicked off the tour for such an antic. But something told me....I just felt it!...that you had a likeness for animals and would understand. You....... youngblood.... are definitely unique in this world."

They hugged.

As Diddley continued to make his way slowly backstage, still sweating with a towel around his neck from Mute, he felt someone tugging on his rear left shoulder. He turned to find Dorethea Doolidge and Sam Bluester as the culprits – Dorethea with a cigarette in her hand and Sam with a drink in his.

"E STAT BELLISSIMO" said Dorethea as she grabbed Diddley and kissed him on the cheek. "That means that was fantastic in Italiano" she said with a laugh, "you are definitely an "eclectic young man and I applaud you for going in your direction – even if it is a new direction. Music needs young souls like you to breathe new life into the genre.....just continue to be you and play and sing from your heart."

"Ditto that!" said Sam, still immaculately dressed with his red-bow-tie and shiny shoes, making sure not to spill his drink, "you sing and play what your soul and heart tells you to play – forget about always trying to make the crowd happy. How does anything ever evolve or change if certain people aren't bold enough to initiate the change – the world would be a stale place and boring as hell. "E STAT BELLISSIMO" or whatever the hell my friend Dorethea just told you. In my language, just keep making it funky young stud" Sam said with a laugh while continuing to ensure he didn't spill his drink.

Didd hugged both Dorethea and Sam Bluester with earnest gratitude....and it came to him that maybe these two were a couple as they walked away in each-other's arms?? "Who cares?" he thought.... they have both been on these road shows for countless years, and now in their twilight years, they deserve to do whatever they want. Moving on down the line toward the backstage rooms.........still wiping the sweat off his face......Didd sees a hoard of musicians headed his way toward the stage. Of course, it is the Treach and Tessa Treu Revue. They have the most musicians – the guitar player with his guitar slung over his shoulder and the bass player with his bass slung over his shoulder – (see - Didd had learned that musicians rarely departed or left their musical instruments out of their sight – YOUR INSTRUMENT WAS YOUR LIVLIHOOD – when it was time to hit the stage, you hit the stage! The roadies and Mute would take care of the microphones and other equipment – but a musician's musical instrument was his pride, joy, and livelihood) so as the musicians passed...next came the back-up singers....and then the other tag-alongs to help get the musicians and back-ups on stage - folks responding to every whim of the headliners. After all - they are the headliners on the tour and Diddley had learned that that's the way the business worked....in a line. If you were more popular and had a bigger fan base – you went on last and closed out the show.

After all these folks passed, Didd could see Tessa Treu shimmying her way down the aisle. She had on this short skirt with glimmers everywhere – but for some reason she didn't seem happy? She had a smile on her face, but Diddley could tell, after all his years with seeing the girls at the Copp-A-Squatt Inn – that something was not right with Tessa.

She paused and spoke to Diddley:

"Diddley – you are destined to be a great performer and spread joy to the world….and to bounce back so effortlessly – and by trying something new? Please continue to believe in your own songwriting skills and to express what you want in your singing and playing. Although it is Ok to listen and take advice from those elders in the music world and those you meet, but in the end, always remember that you are in control of what you say and how you want to say it. The world needs newness, and you can be one of those to spread joy and love. Now I must tell you something quickly before I hit the stage and I trust you will keep this to yourself. That is, Treach is a monster and fears any type of competition! He told the girls and the band members NOT to listen to your set and that if he learned any of them did they would be fired on the spot. Treach is in this business for only himself, and one day maybe I can break away and be free from his slave ways. I never got in the business for this. But, we will have to talk about this later – I've got to get to the stage…….and I have to tell you although I'm going through all this with Treach – my one joy is getting on the stage and performing. It is like a break! I forget all that is happening bad in the world – and in that next hour…. hour and a half – I get to let loose and express myself. And young Didd – what I just heard from you – and yes…. I snuck away and went up top and just listened to your performance – you have true talent that the world needs to hear. So, keep writing your songs and sing what you want – you will have good days and bad days………and remember…. we will talk more in the future."

She then slithered up to Diddley and gave him an innocent kiss on his forehead.

The next thing he heard was this loud "SLAP" and Tessa hitting the floor- CLUNK? Treach, who was initially behind the other band members but who apparently had seen Tessa stop and talk to Didd and ran forward – had slapped the heck out of Tessa on the right side her face – a very vicious slap - all because of the innocent kiss she had given Diddley.

EVERYBODY STOPPED MOVING….and the girls assisted Tessa to her feet.

"BITCH! Don't you ever kiss another man in my presence!' Treach yelled out. He hovered over her and pointed a mean finger. The other girls and band members helped Tessa to her feet. She picked herself off – luckily there was no blood – and they hurried to the stage………..where the chants of "TREACH AND TESSA………..TREACH AND TESSA….were growing.

While the band members, including Tessa, were making their way to the stage – Didd turned around and Treach Treu was directly in his face.

"Diddley Squatt – you kissing my wife you young nothing!' he said as he moved directly into Diddley's face.

"Mr. Treu," said Diddley, in a scared voice, "I was just coming off the stage when your wife Tessa came up to me. All the other performers on this Chitlin Circuit came to wish me good wishes after my performance – and I spoke to each of them and thanked them for their encouragement – and I was doing nothing different when your wife approached me. Sir…. I was doing nothing different!"

'Why did she kiss you? My woman doesn't just kiss anybody? I've taught her better- she doesn't kiss nobody - after being on the road maybe more years that you have even been born! I saw that kiss!" said Treach with fury and spit flailing out of his mouth.

"All she was doing was wishing me well............ did you see me pull her to me? I was just grateful that so many of the performers on this – my first tour- have been supportive of me and my music on my first tour. Plus.... sir, if I can ask you......do you think she would purposely kiss me in public as if we were having an affair – HERE BACKSTAGE IN FRONT OF EVERYBODY? Yes.... I've gotten to know a bunch of the performers on this tour – but I've talked to you and your crew the least of everybody. I'm just trying to learn and spread my wings, whatever they may be. I would never.... never......kiss a man's wife in public. It wasn't even a kiss – she was just wishing me well – jeeezzzz," said Diddley as he finished and attempted to leave back toward the dressing rooms.

"Just a kiss? Is that what you said Diddley? Well let me show you what just a kiss is," said Treach as he TWIRLED AROUND AND HIT DIIDLEY DIRECTLY INTO HIS LEFT EYE- THE OPPOSITE EYE THAT THE CONFEDRATE-FLAG-OVERRAL GUY HAD HIT HIM IN EARLIER!"

Diddley once again hit the ground immediately.....couldn't believe this was happening again? Before anybody could come over to help Diddley, for SOME reason he found the strength to get up on his own......and while Treach had turned his back thinking he had knocked Diddley out......Diddley was on his feet and grabbed TREACH BY THE SHOULDER- AND AS TREACH SURPRISINGLY TURNED AROUND – DIDDLEY TURNED AND THREW HIS RIGHT FIST DIRECTLY AT TREACH'S FACE – MOUTH CENTRAL!"

However

Treach ducked and Diddley's punch went flying into the air unscathed and didn't land anywhere.

"YOU FOOL – YOU DIDN'T KNOW I USED TO BOX WHEN I WAS IN MY TEENS LIKE YOU AND BEFORE I HAD TO TURN TO MUSIC TO HELP SUPPORT MY MOTHER AND THE REST OF MY BROTHERS AND SISTERS? YOU DON'T KNOW SQUATT ABOUT TREACH!", said Treach as he grabbed Diddley and this time SOCKED HIM DEAD INTO THE FOREHEAD! THIS HIT WAS BRUTAL - SENT DIDDLEY TO THE FLOOR IN SECONDS AGAIN!

This time the roadies and all the performers jumped in and grabbed Treach before he could hit Diddley again and pushed him away. Treach huffed away back toward the stage.......and said "Cm'on Treu Review- we got a show to do. But I just want to tell you this before we get on stage........I'm giving you this one reprieve youngblood before I really hurt you, but just don't let me see you ever in my woman's face again. Tessa is my woman.......and I know you are still a young man...with a crazy-ass name of Diddley Squatt....but you need to learn and man up fast. You don't EVER mess with a black's man wife.......even if Diddley don't know Diddley - you gonna learn Squatt in the wrong way. And as for that song you just completed?? - yeah....I listened..... what kind of shit was that? Niggers don't want to hear anything about "rights.......and wrongs....and moments that take your breath away? Nigger please.... negro's wanna hear about a women's backside......and liquor....and dancing the night away. They don't want any type of political shit. I've been doing this for a long time....and what you trying to bring not gonna happen while Treach is playing! So, take your crazy ass book and write you some good loving, smooth ass looking love songs. Shit."

"Band...let's get on stage and give these folks what they want!"

Indeed.... the Treach and Tessa Treu Revue moved toward the stage, although looking back at Diddley and you could tell they were wishing him well - and they had probably seen previous situations with the notorious Treach.

As for Diddley.......

"Diddley - you OK?" said all the performers and roadies as they ran to check on Diddley.

Diddley, eyes closed, could hear the words, and knew he

had been punched a lunch....but he felt all those around them and he felt the love around him. He slowly opened his eyes.

"I'm OK.... what happened?" asked Diddley.

"What happened?" said Slappy Fox.... "you just got teached by the notorious Treach - knocked the shit out of you! Last time the right eye- this time the left. I'm surprised you can see at all! But....at least you stood up for yourself this time......better with a crazy black man than a crazy white man."

"I feel it in my eye and forehead," said Diddley as he was helped to his feet," but I'm alright. What in the world is happening to me with all these fights? I had very few fights at the Copp-A-Squatt growing up.... why all this all of a sudden?"

"It's called learning," said Dorethea," you just learning what a lot of us already went through.... the road is tough. Now - go put some ice on that eye and forehead and you will be OK" as all the other performers nodded and agreed.

Diddley walked down the backstage aisle in hopes to make it back to his dressing room - mixed with the positive reception he received from the crowd but the negative situation he just experienced with Treach.

Sigh.. all the performers had talked so he was ready to get to his room and relax. Right before he got to his door he felt someone pulling on his back leg. He turned around and it was Pee-Wee - or MC Little - all 4ft of him. Didd thought "oh no! what's coming now?" but he graciously stopped and turned around and bent down to talk to Pee-Wee.

Pee -Wee was sharp as usual - funky sharp! He had on his black-and-white stage suit, cufflinks, bow-tie- and of course, his black-and-white pat-and-leather shoes. Pee-Wee only stood about 4 and 1/2 feet tall! But that didn't seem to bother him.

"Young Mr. Diddley Squatt – was I impressed with your performance? I can't lie....it had some holes......but at least you seemed very sincere on stage. And I saw what Treach did to you.....happens often to newbies- hang in there and I'm sure the older performers helped school you. Now..........I've been MC'ing for a long time....and I've witnessed some of the greats.....an although you aren't nearly there yet......I can see some potential. Plus – the other performers on the tour seem to like you so that is a big plus.

As to your performance?" said Pee-Wee as he loosened his bow tie, took off his jacket, relaxed - took off his pat-and- leathers.

"I've seen thousands of musicians and performers as we travel thru this Chitlin Circuit. I know some people may be upset that we have to travel this way – but that's the way of the world now-a-days. In the future, I'm sure black performers will be allowed to travel on jets and planes – you just watch. But anyway – I'm sure some of the earlier performers have told you some of the same words I'm about to say; and that is, - THANK YOU FOR BEING YOURSELF and if you feel it in your heart to bring new style music into this world, that is only natural."

'" I'm 4ft-Shit" – I've been laughed at since I was born. I've been spit on; pissed on; shit on; from everybody – beginning when I was a young student in elementary school.... through middle school.....to high school....not only the students bullying me because of my size – but the teachers also. Everybody, since my birth, since I was bullied all my life because of my size - I would never make it through grade school let alone life. Teachers told me I was shit and never would make it.

However, I found jobs in my city.... picking cotton....... helping out in fields...working in factories. I hated it....my mom thought at least I was working, especially at my disadvantaged height.

But you know what? One day when I was driving - I arrived at a bridge.....and I figured I could just end it all. The bridge wasn't that busy – but cars would come flying up and down. I stopped and looked over the edge of the bridge – ready to jump into the river and end it all so that Pee-Wee, me, didn't have to endure this shit anymore.

So, I am at the bridge.......out in the middle of nowhere USA – looking over the edge of the bridge and I'm ready to just forget my short-ass life by taking a jump. No idea if I would feel pain – but at this point I didn't even care. But just before I figured I would jump..........out of the right side of my eye – I saw a momma turtle trying to cross the street and she had these baby children turtles following in step behind her.....following their mom across the street – just following to get through to the other side. I noticed the last turtle was small as shit.......he was a baby turtle.......and I could tell his brothers and sisters were looking back at him and saying......

" C'mon Pee Wee turtle- we know that we have bullied you and sassed you because you are so young and so small and the runt....but we still love you......you can make it....step it up and join us on the other side......you have to MAKE THIS ON YOUR OWN!?

"And do you know what?" said Pee-Wee," that young turtle strutted straight up and marched with his brothers and sisters across that bridge and they all got safely across that street – right before a car came zooming across. When they were safely across the street – I saw the other turtles come back to Pee-Wee and hug him and show him some love.

So, I'm standing there .... ready to jump.........and I said:

"Fuck this – If Pee-Wee the turtle didn't give up – I will never give up!" and I got in my car and drove home. I've been pushing ever since....and fuck anybody who doesn't think I can be somebody just because of my height or my color – a white guy on a black tour......I'm pushing and so should you. And I told anybody I met after that, that my new name was "PEE-WEE!"

"So, I'm telling you Diddley Squatt - you got some Pee-Wee will in you – young Diddley, and I will support you the rest of the way!"

Pee-Wee and Diddley hugged and Diddley had tears in his eyes from Pee-Wee's words. Pee-Wee moved on down the hall, walking his small body with much respect.

Diddley himself wiped tears from his eyes. He made it to his dressing room and went inside and gently closed the door. While thrilled with his performance and the positive conversations he had with many of his fellow musicians- he was indeed saddened but also happy by the story about Pee- Wee; and indeed, perturbed with the unfortunate situation with Tessa and Treach and getting socked again.

Sly jumped out of his pouch – and ran to the window and got a nut from his area.

Diddley sat on the couch, as Sly grabbed a nut and started gabbing:

"What a night – huh? Please don't tell me you are upset about what that idiot Treach Treu just said and did to you," said Sly as he scratched both of his ears with his hind legs while enjoying his nut. "That guy is what will soon be known as an old-school fool – he can't see that music is changing. Plus, he knows that you new youngbloods with new sounds will push his style out of place and he and his sound will suffer. All things must change!" Sly said and then ran around Diddley's shoulder and got directly into his ear.

"YOU CAN'T STOP CHANGE AND NEW! And as to the fight……. which is I believe your second in a couple of days – hey……. hardheads are everywhere. I've had plenty of fights in my day……. you gotta learn to duck and move……. we had a fighting squirrel back in the day named Cassius……..man could he duck and move" Sly then laughed and jumped on to the table; he did a fighter's duck and move sequence as he squirreled his way around the room…..doing a funky dance in between.

Diddley leaned his head back into the chair....and sighed.

"I don't want to hurt anybody. I'm just trying to express myself like Momma Squatt, and Robert Johnson, and Tiffany, and Chastity – like I promised them all I would do once I got out on my own. They all told me I would run into problems – so I guess this was like an experience and I need to learn from it."

"There you go," said Sly, "use this night as a learning experience and know that not all things will always go your way. Shake off the bad and move on. Do you know how many times I've run'/flew/run through the woods trying to find nuts for me and other folks – and come up empty? Do you think I cried and just gave up? Animals can never give up – hell – we'd be extinct by now if we gave up. The morning is a new day and you get up and try, try again. While I'm talking about squirrels, we had this one other squirrel named MartinL.....we called him MartinLKing – but he would always tell us to never give up in finding food for our families and never forget that animals were brought here through God's kingdom and that while we are here are earth – to always seek freedom and to fight for our rights to hunt for nuts. Martin L. King is somebody I will never forget – and if I'm having a tough day – I just think about him and then I get encouraged and move on. Like.....It's unbelievable you didn't go total bonkers mad at that Treach character tonight. Made me think about two things that I heard MartinL tell us animals one time..........he said:

"DARKNESS CANNOT DRIVE OUT DARKNESS; ONLY LIGHT CAN DO THAT. HATE CANNOT DRIVE OUT HATE; ONLY LOVE CAN DO THAT"

Then he said:

"INJUSTICE ANYWHERE IS A THREAT TO JUSTICE EVERYWHERE"

"That MartinLKing squirrel was a smart animal!"

"So my friend, use this as a positive experience and use it in some future songs....that's what you do......use what you heard on some future songs."

Sly then jumped up top on the couch and said:

"Before you did your song, you talked but you really didn't rap in rhymes – you know what I'm saying? Diddley, listen I'm going to help you out – I'm gonna give you a rap;"

Sly stands on his hind legs and spreads his hands and wings- flying squirrel style. He then starts his "rap:"

"You turn the negative into a positive

the bad into good

and you compose your next song

like MartinLKing would!

You take the good in each day

And you don't take the bad

You watch whatever you say

Cause like Emmitt Till, you could make somebody sad

Life is unknown.......... And

That's just how it be

So be yourself and love everyone

And let your eyes see what they see

This is a rap and the beginning

We gonna move forward with the winning

And Diddley Squatt will be a leader

So, all you squirrels find your feeder

It's a brand-new day in the music world

So just sit back and give young Diddley a twirl!"

Sly then went crazy all over the room......running at amazing speed from one end to the next – stopping to tickle Diddley under his cheek as Diddley let out a laugh....and Sly kept running.

It was quite a night for Diddley. He was so conflicted about the night, that he didn't even bother for a second to go see Treach and Tessa close the show....... just couldn't do it. He got some ice and put it over his swollen eyes and forehead.

Soon both fell asleep..... because, in the morning after breakfast, they would be on their 3-hour bus ride to the great state of Georgia – city Atlanta......and the famous Royal Peacock Theatre.

CHAPTER 8
NEXT STOP #3 – ATLANTA GEORGIA

ROYAL PEACOCK THEATRE

Diddley woke up early the next morning – way too excited to sleep after such a glorious night before. As always, the first thing he did was brush his teeth, as the girls at the Copp-A-Squatt had taught – 2 minutes minimum. Up and down on the bottom – up on the top – down to the bottom gums. Momma Squatt and all the ladies at the Copp- A-Squat had mentored him to ALWAYS spend time brushing your teeth as dental care was very important- especially the radiant smile an entertainer needed when being before an audience or an interviewer……but that wasn't always the case for black performers. While white artists could afford dentists, it was different for blacks. Dental care was unfortunately a big problem among black folks during these times……they just couldn't afford dental care. Many of the performers had terrible teeth, and would often perform their own (or with help from a friend) care and extractions. Luckily for Diddley, his teeth were in excellent condition because of the care he took in brushing early on in life- both in the morning and before bed.

On the bus, heading to the next leg of the Chitlin Tour.

"Alright folks," said W.C, "we all loaded and we got about a 2 and ½ hour/3-hour ride to our next stop to the great state of Georgia – city known as Atlanta. So just sit back and relax….and enjoy the beautiful scenery. Old W.C. will get you there safe and sound – and then it will be up to you to make that special "sound" and make your folks happy," he said with a belly laugh at his "sound" metaphor joke. W.C. slapped his thighs. The engine huffed and puffed………. Atlanta here we come.

"HMMM............... HMMMM............. HUFF!" the "Chitlin Hilton/and or Betty B" began making its way down the highway. The "customary" began: Diddley sat in his "customary" window seat, a bit more in the middle of the bus, and this time gazed out the window. The "customary" oldster musicians/crew in the back (mainly Treach's troop) were falling asleep quickly after passing around the "customary" brown paper sack bottle of liquor-folks taking a morning shot of liquor; and the newly "customary" smoke from this new "weed" marijuana (becoming more and more popular) joint was being puffed-and-passed throughout the rear.

Diddley? He pressed his head against the window and watched as the bus grizzled through the countryside. Sly was asleep in his pouch. As others slept- this was Diddley's time to see the world! As the Betty B chugged through various small cities......and farmlands....and fields.... all Diddley could do was watch and wonder at the land God had made. He of course loved looking at everything – first-of-all the nature: the trees; the tree branches as they reached into the sky and blocked the sunlight off and on; and then the beautiful mountains with their brown skinned scopes and rocky edges as they cascaded down slopes of black and brown and beautiful dirt. This is what Diddley loved! And then, the nature of human beings and animals – God's living creatures; in the fields he could see the workers.... mainly black.... but more and browner skinned immigrants...bending and toiling in the fields, picking out the peanuts, the peaches, pecans, blueberries, ... then still some cotton fields......some watermelon fields.......then the open lands raising cattle cows, and goats ,then horses. And it hit Diddley's mind and he drifted:

THE WORLD IS DIVERSE IN EVERY ASPECT? PEANUTS,

AND COTTON, AND WATERMELON, AND PEACHES - ALL DIFFERENT SHAPES AND COLORS. CATTLE? BROWN-WHITE-BLACK – ALL DIFFERENT COLORS. TREES AND MOUNTAINS? GREEN, BROWN, RUSTY, ORANGE, AND BLACK – ALL DIFFERENT COLORS. AND LASTLY, THE PEOPLE – BLACKS.....WHITES....BROWNS......SOME BORN HERE....OTHER NEW IMMIGRANTS NOW MERGING INTO AMERICA – ALL DIFFERENT SHAPES AND COLORS.

Diddley's mind then drifted back to reality as he thought to himself:

"Ok……I'm on a bus and just left a big white city……and stayed in a hotel and could visit a city with white people walking around. And, look at this now? Most of my people are still out here working in fields……..manual labor……..and I'm playing music to make a living? So…..what can I do? By myself, I can't change the conditions the world is in today? I can't make these folks working in the field maybe get into a college and go to school?.maybe get a degree one day……maybe get a better job and raise their family members, sons and daughters, to maybe have a better life for themselves? So, the best that I can do, is I have to make sure and remember how blessed I am and what I'm doing – and most importantly – remember those who helped me get here. **Maybe one day my life can be an example how maybe to do something different and be successful – but first-off I have to be successful?** I'm lucky."

Diddley tried to break his thought – but his mind kept thinking:

"How does a person even think about having a fun and successful life? These folks in the fields and the mills – maybe they let loose and dance and sing on Friday and Saturday nights………go to church on Sunday……but then Monday hits and it's the same damn thing all over again! How do they do it? Grinding………grinding………. only to live for the weekend and to get a break. How do you think about having a life with a wife and kids? Would you want to bring up your kids in this environment?

Diddley snapped out of it – because he knew he had to remain positive and pushing. He knew what he needed to do, at this point, was to say a prayer to himself……as Momma Squatt and the Girls had taught him – because he needed to keep going on his journey. So, he pulled the tiny Bible he ALWAYS kept with him out of his back pocket….and he remembered the girls had told him Proverbs 17:22. Diddley read to himself:

Oh Lord, my heart is overwhelmed. I'm so frustrated, it is at times difficult to be cheerful and positive. Lord, I fix my eyes upon you. For you have promised you will never leave me nor forsake me. You will bless me with the desire of my heart, as I keep a focus on you. Thank you Lord for your unmerited grace and favor upon my life and your peace that passes all understanding. Thank you for your blessings upon my life daily. In the name of Jesus.....I pray....AMEN!"

Diddley said his "AMENS" secretly and then it was back to looking out the window. Believe it or not – Diddley felt better, as he did after always saying a prayer – he felt more positive that maybe the world could get better for not only black people, but all people, and maybe, by him writing some special songs, he could help the world get better.

Diddley drifted off to sleep.... his head against the window....but his mind a littler clearer.

Later.

"Wake Up – my Chitlin Circuit Family......for we are nearing the famous Royal Peacock Theater in the great southern state of Georgia- city of Atlanta!" came W.C.'s voice. That voice was so recognizable to Diddley by now.

Diddley opened his eyes, and felt refreshed from his earlier prayer. He looked out the window to a bustling downtown area of mainly, again, white folks – but more black folks than the last stop; walking in a busy downtown street – ladies in dresses and men in top hats and suits....... busily walking here and there........kids running around, in and around the bustling sidewalks, black folks with their parents telling them to "slow down." Businesses and cafes on the left and right.... office building doors next to book stores, grocery stores, gift shops, cleaners......some buildings big with various apartment stories....other just one stories crammed in-between the next........downtown cities were exciting looking because of the energy from the streets.

W.C. again:

"The Royal Peacock lies at 186 Auburn Avenue, in what's called the "sweet Auburn" area of Atlanta. We got about a couple of minutes to reach our hotel. Although only the third leg of this part of the Chitlin Circuit Journey - *Atlanta is an important and hot city*. Lots of blacks in this city – and a GREAT opportunity for each of you groups to spread your sounds and maybe get somebody important to hear your music........maybe think about one day signing you to a record contract or something. Also, the Royal Peacock is a MUCH bigger venue than we just left....so don't be surprised by a bigger, noisier crowd. We got in a little early so ya'll have time to check into your hotel rooms and plenty of time to sleep. The concert begins tonight about 8p.m. – so use this slack time wisely. My last bit of advice, as always, is to play well and with intensity. Alright.....here we go.......we at the Sunny Auburn Hotel."

The Betty Boop pulled into the hotel parking lot and Mute and others jumped out first and began unloading the luggage from the side of the Betty B. This hotel was also bigger and better than the last. Mute gave Diddley their version of the new handshake they had invented – called the "high five" – where they both raised their arms over their heads and then came down and slapped hands......... as they both yelled" HIGH FIVE."

Diddley got to his room and Sly couldn't wait to jump out.

"Oh jeeeeeezzz!' said Sly when Diddley let him out of his pouch and Sly jumped out and started running around the room in glee. Sly flew/jumped from the bed, to the drawer, to bathroom, to couch.....just flying around the room in happiness.

"So...you got any snacks for your bestie?' said Sly, "but first open the window......I gotta go take care of my business....be back in a flash.

Diddley opened the window and Sly was gone in a flash....and even back faster.

Diddley pulled out some nuts he had gotten from the machine in the lobby of the hotel and laid them out on the drawer top. Sly ran over and immediately picked up a nut and went to town.

"Oh.... I love my nuts!" he said, "so Mr. Diddley, we made the third city stop of Atlanta. Do you have anything special planned for this third stop?

"I have no idea what is happening next," said Diddley as he fell onto the bed, totally exhausted. He turned over. "I'm taking every step of this experience, minute by minute. I have and will listen to anybody who offers any advice; but eventually, I'm just trying to do the best thing in my mind that comes at the time. I wish I could give you a better answer my best friend.... but I can't. I'm just trying to absorb. But what I am doing, of course, is at the end of the day jotting down stuff that happened that day in my trusted journal like Robert Johnson suggested.

Diddley pulls out his journal and shows it to Sly and jots down some notes.

Sly could tell Diddley had been busy, tinkering within his mind, thinking about the past and the future, and he felt he needed to do something to relax Diddley. So, he ran over to Diddley's shoulder....as Diddley had hugged a pillow under his chin, and he whispered in his ear:

"I have a feeling someone new is going to be entering into your life......somebody new and exciting......and although you (and of course me, with my help) are doing well....we will be doing better and moving ahead stronger. I CAN JUST FEEL IT.... YOU'LL SEE. NOW- ANYMORE NUTS???!!

Sly then laughed and let out a "WHOOOPEEE" as he scattered across the room in glee. Diddley pulled some nuts he had hid from up under his pillow and threw them throughout the room. Sly laughed and scampered - and picked up nuts. That Sly was something else!

Didd needed a nap before tonight's gig. All the things on his mind, but he decided to not let those things bother him. He needed some sleep and they had hours before the show – he just wanted to clear his mind. So he just slept...............and he knew Sly wouldn't bother him. However – he did know – that with his new job and profession, he would have to awake soon and perform on stage. THIS WAS HIS NEW LIFE.

Didd slept well until he felt a lick on his ear. He knew it was Sly and he was trying to tell him something.

"Diddley! Diddley! Wake up....don't you hear somebody knocking on the door!" said Sly as he scampered from one end of the room to the next.

"OK.... I got it," said Didd as he swept his eyes and moved to the door, "I'm up.....I didn't oversleep did I?"

Diddley opens the door and there is this strange looking white dude standing at the door with a shy smile on his face. He is a bit strange looking – first because his hair is a lot longer and curlier than what was worn in the day by white folks. Also – he had a beard growing. He is about Diddley's size.... about Diddley's weight (slim), and he is wearing denim (blue jean) pants and a t-shirt with "I LOVE ALL MUSIC" plastered over the front. He has on sunglasses and tennis shoes........ and he is carrying something in a bag. Diddley always loved tennis shoes and figured to wear them always while performing.

"Can I help you?" said Didd through sleepy eyes.

"Aaaaaaa....yes....so sorry to bother you Mr. Diddley

Squatt – I am so sorry If I awakened you from your sleep. I know how much sleep and rest time is important to a touring musician – but I just had to meet you. My name is Righteous Clemens, and I too am a musician."

"No problem," said Diddley, because once he heard "I too am a musician" he immediately wasn't afraid of this different looking person at his door.

"What can I do for you…..did you say your name is Righteous?" said Diddley.

" Yes…….Righteous Clemens….I'm from Shreveport, Louisiana……..but I've bounced all around the South in my lifetime. The reason for my disturbing you is because me and the band I'm currently jamming with were in Birmingham, Alabama on an off-night last night and I decided to wander over to the Carver Theater because I just love all kinds of music…..and I caught your act. I play keyboards, bass, guitar – just about any instrument you can name. The only way to put it when I heard your music – was I was just blown away! Your music spoke to me……and although it was a long stretch, and my band has a few nights off, I asked around and they told me you were heading to Atlanta….and I didn't care…….I got in my car and I drove all the way to Atlanta in hopes of meeting and talking to you.

"You drove all the way here from Birmingham just to meet me?" said a flabbergasted Diddley.

"Yes I did….that's how much your music and spirit moved me. Once my heart feels the need to do something different and special, well, let's just say I never go against my heart."

"You "never go against your heart." That's an interesting line…….I may have to jot that down and use it in a song one day," said a smiling and laughing Diddley.

"Come on in Righteous – I'm gonna dig meeting you!" said

Diddley as he swept the door open and Righteous walked in with a smile on his face and took a seat in a chair. Diddley sat in a chair across from Righteous.

"So Righteous...you know I'm probably much younger than you....that's why I'm so taken with you showing up at my door. I just love music of all types. And musicians of all types. That's why I let you in. So, what was it that you loved or liked about our last performance? I too love listening to fellow musicians performances?"

"Just the truthfulness in your song lyrics on the original song you sang 'Moments That Take Your Breath Away," said Righteous.

"As I sat at the bar with a drink in my hand....your lyrics just resonated and took me back to my childhood. I actually...you aren't going to believe this – but I closed my eyes as you got deep into your song. I'm a young cat also, maybe not that much older than you, and my parents weren't always around, but my mother especially told me that my rights one day would always outweigh my wrongs. Another thing that really hit me was the song was played a little more bluesier and...I don't know how to describe it.... a little different than just the blues way that we are used to hearing songs? Your guitar playing was a different......more upbeat and twangier – than what you hear on the radio. I remember bumping into an old black guitar player years ago, I think he said his name was Chucky Berries or something along those lines – and he told me that one day soon a new type of music would emerge and he hoped to help introduce it.... more electric.......more of the blues/jazz/gospel merged together.....boogie-woogie something.... "R&B/rhythm and blues" I think....and he said that music at some point would become more "FUNKY."

So, I remember thinking "funky?'

FUNKY???????

Please don't be offended.... but you may be the first funky guitar player I've ever heard in my life.

Maybe that's what encouraged me to drive this far to meet you?

"Funky?????????" said Diddley.

"I LIKE that word Funky" said Diddley as he clapped his hands in unison. He then kept clapping his hands as he repeated the word:

"funky"

"funky"

"funky"

"funky"

"funky"

"funky"

"funky"

"funky"

"funky"

Diddley stood up while clapping and repeating the phrase. At first awkwardly, then happily, righteous stood up with Diddley as they both clapped and continued phrasing:

"funky"

"funky"

"funky"

"funky"

"funky"

"funky"

"funky"

"funky"

"funky"

Finally, after about 3 minutes, Diddley and Righteous fell to the floor exhausted, laughing all the way down......and while on the floor their eyes connected......and Diddley said:

"Righteous - I think I have found a new friend! One day we will definitely get together and jam- we will indeed play that funky music!"

They both smiled at each other and gave the peace sign. Didd had indeed met another new friend.

WHEW!

That night. Day 3 on the Chitlin Circuit Tour- Royal Peacock Theatre in Atlanta, Georgia.

The groups are backstage at the Theater – once again- a much BIGGER club than both the Harlem Duke and the Carver. Slappy Fox opened the show and loosened up the crowd with his bawdy humor and trick-and-treat -of-the-nasty jokes....just loosened them up as usual. Dorethea came on next and enthralled the folks with her operatic beautiful songs. Stan the Lizard Man had folks squirming in their seats – hoping his lizards didn't get loose and run rampant through the crowd. Jack-Leg Batey came next and tapped his ridiculous leg crazy to the crowd's delight. King D.D. slew the crowd with his blues playing, and Sam Bluester joined him as they combined for some downhome blues numbers that had the crowd singing along.

And....to Diddley's surprise, Pee- Wee introduced Treach Treu and the Revue next – which meant Diddley would be closing the show? Now....yes.....Diddley closed the show before but that was just a mistake and a disaster and at a much smaller venue. But this was strange? Diddley thought - Treach was always the headliner and had the ego to prove it – why had he or someone changed the order and decided to come on before Diddley? Strange?

Treach Treu and the Tessa Revue hit the stage and of course the crowd goes wild. The ladies are dressed in sexy shimmered short dresses and they shake everything they got through every song. Tessa is the lead singer and sexy as always – sashaying her way from one end of the stage to the next as she belts out the Review's Chitlin Circuit standards and hits like "Rolling on the High River"...."You a Fool In Love"...."River High – Mountain Deep." Treach always remains in the background, playing his electric guitar and leading the band and occasionally yelling at a bandmate stuff like:

"turn that shit down" ......

" are you playing in the right key motherf*6ss8uker" ......

" you gonna be fined if you don't play better you *&^%$#@@@!"

Treach was notorious for talking to his band while they were on stage during the actual concert.

As the group continues to tear into their repertoire of hits, Diddley is to the side of the stage watching the group perform. As he looks out into the crowd, he happens to catch a glimpse of the guy he had just met last night – Righteous Clemens – sitting in the audience not too far from the stage. He is easy to spot because he is one of the few white people in the audience. He has on his jeans…a nice suit jacket over the top, and is sitting and grooving with a drink in his hand.

Treach and Tessa Treu Revue put on their usual great show, and as their set is nearing its end and Tessa is finishing up the last song and about to the thank the audience…. Treach moves from out the back to the center stage and rudely pushes Tessa out the way and grabs the microphone.

"Ladies and gentlemen, we thank you for coming out tonight and thank you for enjoying our show. Next – about to come to the stage – is this young cat named Diddley Squatt. Before he comes on, it's OK to laugh just because his name is Diddley Squatt and that alone deserves a laugh."

The crowd laughs.

"But I also want to tell you that this young fool also thinks he may be bringing something new into the music world…. like jazz and blues intertwined………something like what the Treach and Tessa Treu Revue world of music you've just appreciated – but this dude thinks he's bringing something new, making music with more "soul" or "R&B" I think I heard him say. Just listen -this young cat is gonna try and hit you with what he thinks is new wave music – like he's a boss or something. But I want to tell you – just listen and don't fall for it! Keep listening to the old stuff…. we invented it. Ain't no new music gonna be taking over soon – unless I invent it. This younger generation has got to learn to respect their elders and that you just can't "hear something" you think is coming from your heart and all of a sudden, the world will change. That's bullshit!"

A few audible groans from the audience.

"So…. once again…. thank you for enjoying our music and our songs – and ladies and gentleman – to close the show – we now present the up and coming, and soon to be world famous superstar – none other than MR. DIDDLEY SQUATT!!' LET'S HEAR THAT

LAUGH AGAIN!

(THE AUDIENCE LAUGHS)

Treach starts laughing and the crowd does laugh – but some people grumble at Treach's crudeness………some clapping, some laughing, some grumbling, some guffawing…….no crowd ever disobeys the famous Treach Treu.

The crowd continues to laugh, applaud – and some disagree – as the musicians exit the stage. The ladies are the first to pass; and Tessa walks up to Diddley and she is NOT happy at all.

"Diddley – I am so, so sorry…. we had no idea that Treach was going to do that. We had no idea we were even going on before you until it happened….and we all wondered what was going on. WHAT IS GOING THROUGH THAT MAN'S MIND? We have no idea why he said what he said about you and your music- which we all love – please understand those are not the ladies or the band's thoughts. I'm getting tired of this man acting out!" Tessa shouted. She had no idea Isaiah was just behind her……and he walked behind her and spun her around.
"**Bitch – you talking about me! I'm the leader of this band and your husband- don't you ever talk bad about me; and especially to a young fool like this young fool. I just kicked his ass last night for you talking, kissing, and messing with him!**" He then slapped her across her face.

The other band members stepped in between the two and stopped any further confrontation. The rest of the ladies grabbed Tessa and helped her to the dressing rooms, but before uttering:

Girls together:

"ENOUGH OF THIS......WE ARE WOMEN.....WE HAVE RIGHTS! YOU CAN'T KEEP DOING THIS!

Girls individually:

"I'm getting tired of this shit."

"Tessa – I don't know how you put up with this man."

"A woman can only take so much. This ain't fair by nobody's means!"

Finally, all the other specific members of the band had left the stage and those familiar with Diddley's music (just about all) remained assembled and tuning up their instruments. The curtains are closed. Strange – but as Diddley began moving to his position on the stage to tune-up his guitar – he noticed these strange piercing eyes behind the right-side curtain. Sure enough, Treach emerged and got right in Diddley's face.

"Alright youngblood. No more punching from me- it ain't needed. We about to see what you can REALLY do before a large crowd - closing. All these folks getting into you and acting like they like your music.... now we really gonna see what you can do having to close the show. I was once in your shoes- and people spit in my face because they didn't like the way I played. You young folks nowadays just think you can talk and sprout about stuff – but you never had the responsibility of CLOSING a show – which means you better be good!

"I just have to ask again- what did I ever do to you?' Diddley said somewhat afraid, but not totally.

"'It's your breed – respect your elders!" slammed Treach.

"But I've never uttered one bad word about you or your group....my grandmother and others brought me up to respect your elders," said Diddley.

"You may not have said anything....... but it's your actions. You think I don't know who your grandmother is? Momma Squatt?? That old bitch that runs that ......what she call it – "Copp-A-Squatt Inn" in Rundown, Mississippi? She's a bitch with a capital B – so is your momma and your daddy. Your momma Jackie was a prostitute and your daddy Doodley Squatt was a pimp – I FUCKED YOUR MAMA!" shouted Treach right in Diddley's face.

Diddley's eyes opened wide – he quickly said to himself "Oh lord – contain me" – it took EVERY muscle/vein/strength in Diddley's heart not to go absolutely insane on Treach – but he held in.

"So, yeah, I know all I need to know about you......my question is what are you doing being nice to my wife and talking to my wife the way you do....and being such good friends with all the other performers on this tour?"

"I like people," said Diddley, still shyly, still sweating, still grasping each breath controllably. He then said with measured gusto, " I've always loved to listen to what people, especially older people, tell me about what they have learned and seen. I didn't attend a lot of school- so I like to listen and talk to people......and animals – and I learn that way. That's how I fell in love with music – and why I am where I am today."

"What do you mean you talk and listen to animals?" said Treach with a strange look on his face.

" Oh.... nothing....by that...I was just kidding" said Diddley. No way in the world was he going to say or explain his relationships with Sly or any of the animals from the days back at the Copp-A-Squatt Inn.

"So, this is it! You closing the show. This is without question your biggest show of your life about to happen after what- just your first couple of shows you ever done? And the thing is – we purposely didn't leave you a lot of time left before these shitty promoters will have to close the show – all events and shows in Atlanta have to stop at 12pm midnight. It's 30 minutes until 11pm. right now…. you got about **an hour and a 1/2** to entertain these folks and show them what you got. HA! (Treach takes a small bottle of whiskey from his pocket and drinks the entire bottle down to the last drop right in Diddley's face.)"

He then let's out a disgusting burp/belch:

"BUUUUUUUUUUUUUUUUUUUURRRRRRRPPPPP PPP BEEELLLCCCCH"

"Show em your new sound," Treach says as he pulls up his pants from the belt-buckle, and struts off the stage laughing.

The band is set. Diddley notices that all the performers who performed earlier- are back and seated on both sides backstage…….probably waiting to see how Diddley handles being unduly embarrassed by Treach Treu…..and…..they just have to stay and see how he handles this important step in his young career.

Seated to the left of the stage:

King D.D.

Treach Treu and the rest of the Revue (including Tessa-Treach with a huge SMIRK on his face)

Stan the Lizard Man

Dorethea Doolidge

Seated to the right of the stage:

Slappy Fox

Jack Leg Batey

Sam Bluester

Before opening the curtains or making a final act announcement, Pee-Wee steps backstage and says in Diddley's ear only:

"Young Diddley – don't let what Treach Treu said mess with your mind. I've seen that a thousand times- me and all the other performers you see hanging back - fools like him try to intimidate the newbies and thinks that will make him look better. Many of them have been in your shoes. You just continue to be you. However, in lieu of saying that youngblood and wishing you the best of luck, I do have to ask you what songs are you playing tonight? I've still got my job to do and introduce you as the final act tonight - and the clock is ticking."

Diddley closes his eyes and does a quick prayer in his mind:

"Lord – help me at this crossroads in my career. Let me show strength and finish out tonight's performance for the good of my Chitlin Circuit team – most of whom have been very supportive of my career. Help me though this Lord.... yes............I hear you Lord......I too believe we should just have fun and do something different.... that's always an escape for me....just let it flow. Thank you, Lord!"

Diddley, just before the curtains are about to rise:

"OK Pee-Wee......let me have a quick word with the other performers before you introduce us. And you can just tell the crowd that the final act is Diddley Squatt from Rundown, Mississippi, just jamming with all the acts you just heard.....just playing.....call it "FUNKING WITH THEIR HEARTS."

"WHAT? You sure," said Pee-Wee with this quizzical look on his face.

"I've never been more sure….just give me a minute or two," said Diddley with determination. He then ran over to the other performers still seated backstage and asked them to gather around:

"You guys are my family," says Diddley while eyeing each and every member of the tour………all there, including the Treach & Tessa Treu Revue except Treach who has left for some reason. "I just want you all to know how much I appreciate and love you all for mentoring me. Is it OK if I ask you all to help me through this finale? I'll just call you – and you can just step on stage – and adlib something along with the music? It will be fun."

They all looked perplexed? Stan looked at Doreathea, Slappy looked at Jack-Leg, King D.D. looked at Sam, and Tessa and the girls looked at Diddley – and then they all looked at Doreathea. Doreathea spoke for everyone and said:

"WELL….I GUESS…. OK YES – WE WILL ALL TRY SOMETHING NEW"

Diddley then is hit by a nut on the top of his head? He looks up…….AND SURE ENOUGH THERE IS SLY SITTING ON A TOP CURTAIN RAIL – HIDDEN FROM ALL – EXCEPT DIDDLEY? Sly then puts his paws together and makes a "HEART SIGN" – and Diddley knows it means "LOVE" from is best friend……..no way Sly wanted but the best seat possible for what was about to happen.

Diddley looked up to Sly and put his hands together in a heart sign…..that silly squirrel!

Diddley, with his guitar strapped around his shoulder, then turned to all the performers seated to the side, gave them all a 2 fingers up peace sign with a gigantic smile on his face, and said "OK….Pee – Wee – LET'S GET THIS PARTY STARTED!"

Pee – Wee, as the curtains open fully:

"Ladies and gentlemen, tonight the world-famous Royal Peacock Theatre from the great city of Atlanta, Georgia is excited to introduce to you a new talent, and he is closing a major show for the very first time - a young fella by the name of Diddley Squatt.

Laughter from the crowd

I know that is a different sounding name; however, it is his real name. It never gets boring introducing this young man – which I'm proud to do since we just started this year's tour. Now, Diddley was born in Rundown, Mississippi and raised and brought up at the famous Copp-A-Squatt Inn. His name is unique. And, I think that you would agree with me – that none of us had the choice to name any of us; that was up to our mommies and daddies. However, this is this cat's real name. And I just want you all to know, that during only the very short time I've grown to know him, while he's been on this most recent tour of the famous Chitlin Circuit and he's only done one or two prior performances, I've grown to love the dude! I've been on this tour for over 30 years – but I'm here to let you all know that this young man is respectful of his elders; respectful of all those folks he meets. You can even laugh at his name – and you know what? He will laugh with you…..doesn't care – as long as you listen to his music. He will tell you as long as you listen to his music- maybe you don't like it – but just thanks for listening to it and giving it a try. And here is a secret that I want you to know – his first guitar hero was none other than Robert Johnson – yes the famous Robert Johnson – who Didd met earlier in his life and who gave him a few guitar lessons.

I've said enough about our next performer. But I do have to let you know you are in for something special about to happen....... Diddley Squatt has informed me that tonight he and the band, and others who join him on stage, will just be "jamming and improvising" for the next hour. That's right – no standard tunes – they will just play what they feel and hope you groove along. I've never heard of this type closing happening before- so I'm as excited as everybody here should be. So.... without further adieu, please welcome to the stage Diddley Squatt on guitar and any other performers and thangs that may happen tonight, as they jam to a song along the lines of "YOU NEVER GO AGAINST YOUR HEART." Ladies and gentleman...
....

Diddley Squatt!"

Pee-Wee spreads his arms. Diddley steps to the center microphone. The crowd is indeed a bit confused on this closing for the Chitlin Circuit Tour- which many have seen MANY times – but can't believe that the famous Treach Treu has given over the closing spot to someone they have never heard play before.

Diddley comes to the microphone and almost knocks it over – obviously a bit nervous of what has transpired:

The crowd is deftly silent and perplexed.

"First off – I want to give a shout out to you folks of Atlanta for coming to see these wonderful performers who put on a great show tonight. We appreciate it. I'm not a big talker – and I know you all already know my name.

Laughs from the crowd.

I just want to say how blessed I am to be on this tour and to have met my fellow musicians. That's why tonight – we are going to close this show with something totally different. It's called freestyle.... it's called "jamming" ....we are all just going to just get a groove going and because all these musicians and earlier performers are so great and talented – we are just going to create for the next hour. None of us know how this is going to happen – or how it is going to turn out. But this is the thing – we are willing to try something different. I am new- this experiment could end my career before it even starts. I keep a journal and I write down things I see. Just last night I met someone and he said a phrase to me which I wrote down and which I am using for tonight.... he told me "You Never Go Against Your Heart." So, yes....... this jamm/song was just written last night. See, before falling asleep last night, I thought about that phrase over and over......

"You Never Go Against Your Heart."

I just thought.... music comes from the soul – which comes from the heart. I never sing, or play anything on my guitar, until it comes from the heart. I want to give to the world all my best from inside of me. So I'm going to spit out some stuff that's straight feelings......and this is important.... once we get a groove going........I'M GOING TO INVITE MY FRIENDS/FELLOW PERFORMERS ON STAGE AND MAYBE SOMEBODY IN THE CROWD TO COME JOIN ME ONSTAGE AND WE ARE JUST GOING TO LET IT FLY – STRAIGHT FROM OUR HEARTS. I hope they are OK with this.

(gasps from the crowd at the idea Diddley just proposed)

One last thing before we get started on this experiment from the heart – there are a lot of terrible things happening today not only in America, but all over the world. We have unfortunate racial problems in our country, and it makes my heart bleed that black people, and people of color in general, are suffering….that any people are denied human privileges – just because of the color of the skin – which NO ONE has control of at birth? Black people fighting for basic civil rights……voting rights?….working rights?…… why??? The one thing I want to add before we get started – is that I want you all to know out there that it isn't just black folks fighting for change – there are some of our white brothers standing up and fighting for us also,

(Some applause, as well as some grumbles from the crowd.)

To me – that means just play what you feel and let it go……go free! So that's what we are doing tonight – just going free. We hope you like it……but????????? ENOUGH TALKING – LET'S GET TO FUNKING!"

Diddley counts off:

"1………2…….3……4… HIT ME DRUMMER!"

The drummer kicks that bass drum and starts the funky beat that is known throughout the land…..just a basic beat that grabs the attention of any crowd.

(drums) "BA BA BA BOOM"

(drums) "CHUCKA CHUCKA"

(drums) "BA BOOM"

(drums) "CHUCKA CHUCKA"

    Diddley allows it to go on for a couple of minutes as the crowd starts to immediately get into it – and the drummer starts to improvise various beats. Drums are the basic bottom of music- you have to have that good beat. Like any musician or concert, the drummer gets into deeper and more different as the crowd gets louder and louder and applauds him along; waiting for some other instrument to join the song. In music- it's like a team. One player starts it – and the rest of the players realize what's going on and join in because it takes an entire team to eventually bring it all home.

(drums) "BA BA BA BOOM"

(drums) "CHUCKA CHUCKA"

(drums) "BA BOOM"

(drums) "CHUCKA CHUCKA"

    A couple of more drummer licks and then the keyboard player lays down a layer of chords across the drumbeat. Now – tonight – what luck? Instead of the usual piano – would you believe the Chitlin Circuit substituted an electric organ into the lineup and it was up to the musician what he wanted to play? Piano's with microphones were great....but this new electric organ was something else! Electric music. The chords and pipes could kick a mule's ass – and so the keyboardist was thrilled to try out this new instrument. As the drummer kicked it – the organist bumped/flicked/licked it!

(organ) "SHACKA LACKA LACKA"

(organ) "SHACKA LACKA LACKA"

(organ) "SHACKA LACKA LACKA"

(organ) "SHACKA LACKA LACKA"

(drums) "BA BA BA BOOM"

(drums) "CHUCKA CHUCKA"

(drums) "BA BOOM"

(drums) "CHUCKA CHUCKA"

That electric organ was blowing unlike heard before – and the crowd soon took notice that this might be a special night alright.

Next it was time for the guitar to kick in – and who better to add to this new funk sound than Sir Diddley Squatt himself. Diddley moved to center stage and before playing one note on his guitar; turned up the amplifier to full blast. Then……..right in time with the drummer and organist, Diddley began on his guitar:

(guitar) "RING DINGA LINGA FINGA

(guitar) "RING DINGA LINGA FINGA

(guitar) "RING DINGA LINGA FINGA

(guitar) "RING DINGA LINGA FINGA

Diddley struck some high guitar licks with his pick terrifyingly picking - that were in tune with the jam......and he repeated these chords.......and the trio of drums, keyboards, and guitar was soon in sync.

(drums) "BA BA BA BOOM"

(organ) "SHACKA LACKA LACKA"

(drums) "BOOM"

(organ) "SHACKA LACKA LACKA"

(drums) "BOOM"

(organ) "SHACKA LACKA LACKA"

(drums) "BOOM"

(organ)　"SHACKA LACKA LACKA"

(guitar) "RING DINGA LINGA FINGA

(guitar) "RING DINGA LINGA FINGA

(guitar) "RING DINGA LINGA FINGA

(guitar) "RING DINGA LINGA FINGA

(so now its)

(drums) "BA BA BA BOOM"

(organ)　"SHACKA LACKA LACKA"

(guitar) "RING DINGA LINGA FINGA

(drums) "BOOM"

(organ)　"SHACKA LACKA LACKA"

(guitar) "RING DINGA LINGA FINGA

(drums) "BOOM"

(organ)　"SHACKA LACKA LACKA"

(guitar) "RING DINGA LINGA FINGA

(drums) "BOOM"

(organ) "SHACKA LACKA LACKA"

(guitar) "RING DINGA LINGA FINGA

(drums) "BOOM"

(organ) "SHACKA LACKA LACKA"

(guitar) "RING DINGA LINGA FINGA

The crowd is enjoying as the trio's simple jam continues to funk and mesmerize. Diddley, without losing a beat.... moves to the microphone and says………"Alright…….GIVE ME SOME BOTTOM!" The bass player now playing an electric bass, which was becoming popular jumps center stage and lays down a funky bass riff:

"RUMP RUMPA RUMPA PUMP"

"RUMP RUMPA RUMPA PUMP"

"RUMP RUMPA RUMPA PUMP"

"RUMP RUMPA RUMPA PUMP"

"RUMP RUMPA RUMPA PUMP"

"RUMP RUMPA RUMPA PUMP"

"RUMP RUMPA RUMPA PUMP"

So now it's the four:

(drums) "BOOM"

(organ) "SHACKA LACKA LACKA"

(guitar) "RING DINGA LINGA FINGA

(bass) "RUMP RUMPA RUMPA PUMP"

(drums) "BOOM"

(organ) "SHACKA LACKA LACKA"

(guitar) "RING DINGA LINGA FINGA

(bass) "RUMP RUMPA RUMPA PUMP"

(drums) "BOOM"

(organ) "SHACKA LACKA LACKA"

(guitar) "RING DINGA LINGA FINGA

(bass) "RUMP RUMPA RUMPA PUMP"

(drums) "BOOM"

(organ) "SHACKA LACKA LACKA"

(guitar) "RING DINGA LINGA FINGA

(bass) "RUMP RUMPA RUMPA PUMP"

Diddley let's the foursome continue to find their groove………various players starting to improvise and throw licks in-between the funky groove. Once again, while the groove continues, Diddley steps center stage and bellows:

"Hope ya'll like the beat we got going now. Isn't it nice?'

The crowd yells back:

"YES………………..KEEP IT COMING……YOU ARE STARTING TO GROOVE!"

"Alright…. alright………..alright!" Diddley repeats with a smile on his face.

"Just remember that all this is improvised – we didn't practice any of this before the show. We have no idea how this is going to turn out – but we won't stop until we feel it is the end.   So now of course we need that final piece……..that final ingredient to add to the gumbo….to make this sound extra special and delicious. Of course, I'm talking about the horns. We got a trumpet player, a saxophone player, and an instrument that the world may not label a horn but you do blow into it……I'm of course talking about the harmonica. So, horns……. are ya'll going to come join the party or what?"

The three musicians run onto center stage and the sax man lifts his horn and is the first to funky honk:

"HONK…A HONK…A HONKA HONK HONK!"

"HONK…A HONK…A HONKA HONK HONK!"

"HONK…A HONK…A HONKA HONK HONK!"

"HONK…A HONK…A HONKA HONK HONK!"

The trumpet is next…..this dude slyly raises his trumpet and kisses his lips….and then blasts:

"TRINK..ATRINK..ATRINKA TRINK TRINK!"

"TRINK..ATRINK..ATRINKA TRINK TRINK!"

"TRINK..ATRINK..ATRINKA TRINK TRINK!"

"TRINK..ATRINK..ATRINKA TRINK TRINK!"

Then the last musician on stage……this super FAT guy by

the name of Barpo, WEARING THIS BEANIE HAT – moves to center stage and puts his harmonica to his lips and blasts like no harmonica ever before :

"HEMM...DEM...ADEM..ADEM DEM"

"HEMM...DEM...ADEM..ADEM DEM"

"HEMM...DEM...ADEM..ADEM DEM"

"HEMM...DEM...ADEM..ADEM DEM"

So that's it! The last musician kicked in and the funky beat is rocking unlike anything else before....I mean the sound is INSANE. The final sound beat continues and it gets funkier by the minute as the musicians latch onto the chords and beats and they add their funkiness in-between – which is what music is all about. The beat is ready....Diddley let's the beat get steady for 3 or 4 minutes – and obviously these seasoned musicians are locked in. This will be the beat for the 45 minutes – with solo spots opened up – but this is it. Get it baby!:

(drums) "BA BA BA BOOM"

(organ) "SHACKA LACKA LACKA"

(drums) "BOOM"

(organ) "SHACKA LACKA LACKA"

(drums) "BOOM"

(organ) "SHACKA LACKA LACKA"

(drums) "BOOM"

(organ) "SHACKA LACKA LACKA"

(guitar) "RING DINGA LINGA FINGA

(guitar) "RING DINGA LINGA FINGA

(guitar) "RING DINGA LINGA FINGA

(guitar) "RING DINGA LINGA FINGA

(bass) "RUMP RUMPA RUMPA PUMP"

(bass) "RUMP RUMPA RUMPA PUMP"

(bass) "RUMP RUMPA RUMPA PUMP"

(bass) "RUMP RUMPA RUMPA PUMP"

(sax) "HONK…A HONK…A HONKA HONK HONK!"

(sax) "HONK…A HONK…A HONKA HONK HONK!"

(sax) "HONK…A HONK…A HONKA HONK HONK!"

(sax) "HONK…A HONK…A HONKA HONK HONK!"

(trumpet) "TRINK..ATRINK..ATRINKA TRINK TRINK!"

(trumpet) "TRINK..ATRINK..ATRINKA TRINK TRINK!"

(trumpet) "TRINK..ATRINK..ATRINKA TRINK TRINK!"

(trumpet) "TRINK..ATRINK..ATRINKA TRINK TRINK!"

(harmonica) "HEMM...DEM...ADEM..ADEM DEM"

(harmonica) "HEMM...DEM...ADEM..ADEM DEM"

(harmonica) "HEMM...DEM...ADEM..ADEM DEM"

(harmonica) "HEMM...DEM...ADEM..ADEM DEM"

Diddley steps to the microphone and says:

"Ok....so we got our funky beat going. So now we need to add some words and vocals to keep this experiment going. So I said we are going to name this jam and song "You NEVER GO Against Your Heart." Since I started this mess.....let me let you know a little about why and I came up with this title. See:

"I like to think about the future and how new genres of music, and the progression, all came to be. First off – everything new is born from something old- ya'll hearing me? Today's black man's music was first brought over from slaves from Africa and what they heard in Africa, probably first from African "churches" – and then they started humming and singing songs to get by while working in the American cotton fields. Black folks music was born. "Gospel" from the early black churches was born from what folks sang in the fields. "Blues" was then hatched from these gospel songs; "Be-Bop" was then hatched from the songs of the blues; "jazz" was hatched from "Be-Bop;" "Rhythm and Blues" – the newest sound coming up next, will then be hatched from Jazz; and the same with white people's music; white people's church music birthed "Country music"; then "Rock and Roll" was birthed from both the blues and country music.

"So now – I'm about to add some words to this funky backbeat that is playing. I won't "sing" the words as in a song, but I'm going to "rap" this words. I'm sure one day this new form of music…..I dunno…..maybe they will call it "ranting"……..or maybe "rapping" – will become a new genre of music. Here goes – let me hear that beat one more time:

(drums) "BA BA BA BOOM"

(organ) "SHACKA LACKA LACKA"

(drums) "BOOM"

(organ) "SHACKA LACKA LACKA"

(drums) "BOOM"

(organ) "SHACKA LACKA LACKA"

(drums) "BOOM"

(organ) "SHACKA LACKA LACKA"

(guitar) "RING DINGA LINGA FINGA

(guitar) "RING DINGA LINGA FINGA

(guitar) "RING DINGA LINGA FINGA

(guitar) "RING DINGA LINGA FINGA

(bass) "RUMP RUMPA RUMPA PUMP"

(bass) "RUMP RUMPA RUMPA PUMP"

(bass) "RUMP RUMPA RUMPA PUMP"

(bass) "RUMP RUMPA RUMPA PUMP"

(sax) "HONK...A HONK...A HONKA HONK HONK!"

(sax) "HONK...A HONK...A HONKA HONK HONK!"

(sax) "HONK...A HONK...A HONKA HONK HONK!"

(sax) "HONK...A HONK...A HONKA HONK HONK!"

(trumpet) "TRINK..ATRINK..ATRINKA TRINK TRINK!"

(trumpet) "TRINK..ATRINK..ATRINKA TRINK TRINK!"

(trumpet) "TRINK..ATRINK..ATRINKA TRINK TRINK!"

(trumpet) "TRINK..ATRINK..ATRINKA TRINK TRINK!"

(harmonica) "HEMM...DEM...ADEM..ADEM DEM"

(harmonica) "HEMM...DEM...ADEM..ADEM DEM"

(harmonica) "HEMM...DEM...ADEM..ADEM DEM"

(harmonica) "HEMM...DEM...ADEM..ADEM DEM

Diddley starts his rap:

"I AM NOT A POET - NOT A SKILLED TALKER- NOT A GENIUS MAN

BUT I LIKE TO WRITE – IT MAKES ME HAPPY- AND SO I DO THE BEST I CAN

THIS IS ALL NEW –YOU WON'T HEAR SINGING – I'LL TALK ALL THE WORDS

IT IS CALLED RAP – I'LL SAY SOMETHING - UNLIKE YOU'VE EVER HEARD

I ALWAYS THINK ABOUT GOOD – I TRY TO NEVER THINK ABOUT BAD

I ALWAYS THINK WHAT MAKES ME HAPPY – NEVER WHAT MAKES ME SAD

LET ME TELL YOU A LITTLE HISTORY – ABOUT THE HUMAN BODY

AND THE PARTS OF IMPORTANCE – NO MENTION OF THE SHODDY

THE HEAD IS AT THE TOP – AND IT HOLDS OUR HUMAN BRAIN

THE BRAIN IS IMPORTANT- BUT IN THE CHEST IS THE HUMAN MAIN

YOUR HEART IS IN THE MIDDLE – AND THAT, FOR SURE, IS FOR A REASON

CUZ YOUR HEART IS ALWAYS BEATING- FROM SEASON TO SEASON

YOUR BRAIN GOES UP AND DOWN, IT CAN BE FUZZY-SWEET-MAYBE TART

YOUR FEELINGS GO BACK AND FORTH – BUT NEVER AGAINST YOUR HEART

SO, THE BODY CAN BE JINGLE JANGLED – YOUR MIND GOES CRAZY NUTS

BUT NEVER GO AGAINST YOUR HEART – IT'S BETTER THAN YOUR GUTS

YOU NEVER GO AGAINST YOUR HEART, NEVER GO AGAINST YOUR HEART

TO START EACH DAY WITH A SMILE, NEVER GO

AGAINST YOUR HEART

LIFE IS UNPREDICTABLE, AND YOU CAN STOP – BUT THEN RE-START

YOU CAN GO-UP-AND DOWN IN LIFE – BUT NEVER AGAINST YOUR HEART

SO, LET ME END MY FIRST RAP, AND I'M GLAD EVERYONE IS STAYING

YOU NEVER GO AGAINST YOUR HEART – YA'LL HEAR WHAT I'M SAYING!"

The crowd goes wild after Diddley completes his first rant/rap of this improvised jam. Diddley appreciates the applause and lets the funky beat proceed. He then moves to the microphone again:

"So now I want to ask the people most dear to me on this, my first tour, to come up and improvise something from their heart. I am so lucky and blessed........ and have learned so much from my Chitlin Tour family....and I understand if maybe what I am asking is too much. I just thought I'd give it a try – they know my mind never stops thinking about new and different stuff......so............Mr. King D.D.......with this funky beat blowing in back of us.........can you maybe....just maybe.......come to the stage once again and tell us your thoughts on what "You Never Go Against Your Heart" means to you?

The crowd starts a slow chant:

"C'MON KING D. D....SHOW US WHAT YOUR HEART MEANS:

SHOW US WHAT YOUR HEART MEANS:

SHOW US WHAT YOUR HEART MEANS:

To the Chitlin Crew Performers seated to the left and the right of the stage, it seemed somewhat surprising as King D.D. rose from his seat WITH NO FEAR, strapped his guitar around his neck, and walked to the stage. He plugged in his guitar and moved to the microphone.

KING D.D.:

"Folks……I've never done this new thing where people get on stage and just improvise either singing or playing. However, for this young blood Diddley Squatt, who we all have grown to love, to admire his spirit, creativity, and tenacity………I'mma give it a shout. Let my guitar sing first:

GUITAR: "twang…twang…. a twang a twang twang!

twang…twang…. a twang a twang twang!

GUITAR: "twang…twang…. a twang a twang twang!

twang…twang…. a twang a twang twang!

King D.D. Sings: "I'm a blues singer and guitarist,

And I don't improvise like this at the start

GUITAR: "twang…twang….a twang a twang twang!

twang…twang….a twang a twang twang!

King D.D. Sings: And although I may be an old dude,

I never go against my heart!

GUITAR: "twang…twang….a twang a twang twang!

twang…twang….a twang a twang twang!

King D.D. Sings: "So, I won't take up a lot of your time

Cause as an old fart I'm not great at rhyme"

GUITAR: "twang…twang….a twang a twang twang!

twang…twang….a twang a twang twang!

King D. D. Sings: "But for my friend Diddley Squatt who is true

King D.D. is in your corner and you do what you do!"

GUITAR: "twang…twang….a twang a twang twang!

twang…twang….a twang a twang twang!

THE CROWD GOES WILD AT KING D.D.'S QUICK/IMPROVISED SET

King D.D. bows – but does not exit the stage. He continues to play along with the funky beat?

"Thank you, King, D.D.!" shouts Diddley as the crowd continues to clap. Obviously, they enjoyed the King's quick words, and jam.

"Next………if you are willing….I bring to the stage the incredible Stan the Lizard Man…..who…..I dunno? Stan…..just do something that shows in your show that "You Never Go Against

Your Heart?"

Stan, who has got to be close/in his 60's, doesn't shy away or go against his heart. He leaves from his seat behind the stage and gestures to his animal handlers to bring him something......no idea exactly what he wants them to bring him that could pertain to an improvise set?

Stan moves to the center stage and his handler's leave two cages to the left and right of his seat. Stan reaches into one of the cages and brings out a huge cobra snake - a beautiful brown and black color as the cobra snakes back and forth as it settles around Stan's neck and chest area. Stan speaks:

"I love that young Mr. Diddley Squatt asked me to participate in this show. He is a young man of great talent and spirit......great generosity. While I may not be a musician like my longtime friends on the tour, you better believe that all my animal friends – including snakes and lizards- all have hearts and they too never go against their heart! They just love to put on a show.......

"And with that being said?"……………………..Stan stands and the cobra continues to snake around his body and Stan breaks into a dance as the funky groove continues as King D.D.'s guitar is added to the funky beat. Stan, while dancing to the beat and the cobra twirling, then bends down and opens the other cage. These huge lizards DANCE out of the box all over Stan's head and the rest of his body......the lizards – some small and some large – of all colors - are even dancing and romping over the cobra snake; but the cobra doesn't seem to mind- it's as if he has welcomed his lizard friends to the party?

King D.D. stands next to Stan, playing his guitar, as they both jam to the music:

(drums) "BA BA BA BOOM"

(organ) "SHACKA LACKA LACKA"

(drums) "BOOM"

(organ) "SHACKA LACKA LACKA"

(drums) "BOOM"

(organ) "SHACKA LACKA LACKA"

(drums) "BOOM"

(organ) "SHACKA LACKA LACKA"

(guitar) "RING DINGA LINGA FINGA

(guitar) "RING DINGA LINGA FINGA

(guitar) "RING DINGA LINGA FINGA

(guitar) "RING DINGA LINGA FINGA

(bass) "RUMP RUMPA RUMPA PUMP"

(bass) "RUMP RUMPA RUMPA PUMP"

(bass) "RUMP RUMPA RUMPA PUMP"

(bass) "RUMP RUMPA RUMPA PUMP"

(sax) "HONK...A HONK...A HONKA HONK HONK!"

(sax) "HONK...A HONK...A HONKA HONK HONK!"

(sax) "HONK...A HONK...A HONKA HONK HONK!"

(sax) "HONK...A HONK...A HONKA HONK HONK!"

(trumpet) "TRINK..ATRINK..ATRINKA TRINK TRINK!"

(trumpet) "TRINK..ATRINK..ATRINKA TRINK TRINK!"

(trumpet) "TRINK..ATRINK..ATRINKA TRINK TRINK!"

(trumpet) "TRINK..ATRINK..ATRINKA TRINK TRINK!"

(harmonica) "HEMM...DEM...ADEM..ADEM DEM"

(harmonica) "HEMM...DEM...ADEM..ADEM DEM"

(harmonica) "HEMM...DEM...ADEM..ADEM DEM"

(harmonica) "HEMM...DEM...ADEM..ADEM DEM"

KING D.D's GUITAR: "twang...twang....a twang a twang twang!

twang...twang....a twang a twang twang!

KING D.D.'s GUITAR: "twang...twang....a twang a twang twang!

twang...twang....a twang a twang twang!

Stan and King D.D. share the stage as the groove continues – Stan dancing crazy, "unlike" an old man while the snakes slither and prance to the beat – D.D. slinging his guitar licks. The crowd loves it! Diddley lets it go on for a couple of minutes before moving back to center stage and taking control of the microphone. The funk beat lowers, but the funk beats continues – in respect of Diddley's next move at the mic.

"WOW……let's hear it for Stan and King D.D.!" shouts Diddley.

Roadies run out and put all the lizards back into their cages. Stan and Kind D.D. wrap their arms around each other's shoulders and bow at center stage – and both then exit.

THE CROWD GOES WILD

Diddley Continues:

"Now…….if my Princess is willing….I'd like to hear something from the great Doreathea Doolidge – one of the greatest black opera singers of our day. Doreathea has been so nice and encouraging to me on this my first tour. Doreathea – I know this beat is a little bit – actually quite a bit- different from anything operatic. However, you have been such an inspiration to me…….maybe you can just come to the stage and sing anything that comes to your mind about "NEVER GOING AGAINST YOUR HEART."

Doreathea – seated to the left of the stage with the others…..at first looks a little skeptical. Now we must understand, opera is not to be played around with! It is a strict genre and style of music and singing and playing, and there is NEVER anything improvisational about it. Doreathea sits there awhile……..and takes a deep breath…..but then rises from the left of the backstage and starts walking toward Diddley and the front. She has a proud look about her! Diddley let's out a smile you wouldn't believe. Doreathea arrives at center stage – the band still laying down the funky groove.

Diddley: "I am so proud and honored that you've accepted this improvised idea of mine...I would not have been unhappy if you didn't want to do this. But.....here you are.....you are a true queen. Doreathea – just get into the beat and add anything you like....as you ALL have told me – THERE ARE NO MISTAKES! This is just having fun with music and nature....thank you my Princess! So band........let's slow the beat down the beat a bit......but please.........KEEP IT FUNKY! Like some funky classical?"

Indeed .....the beat slows.....but it is a funky slow.

Doreathea at the microphone: "Diddley Squatt – you are indeed a unique individual. I am so honored to be present in this, a major step in your life, and yes, while I don't do many improvised spots- I am indeed going to help you out. You promise me to just continue to do you, Diddley Squatt, and let's see what I can do.....now move out the way youngster!"

The funky slower beat continues:

(drums) "BA BA BA BOOM"

(organ) "SHACKA LACKA LACKA"

(drums) "BOOM"

(organ) "SHACKA LACKA LACKA"

(drums) "BOOM"

(organ)   "SHACKA LACKA LACKA"

(drums) "BOOM"

(organ)   "SHACKA LACKA LACKA"

(guitar) "RING DINGA LINGA FINGA

(guitar) "RING DINGA LINGA FINGA

(bass)   "RUMP RUMPA RUMPA PUMP"

(bass)   "RUMP RUMPA RUMPA PUMP"

(sax) "HONK...A HONK...A HONKA HONK HONK!"

(sax) "HONK...A HONK...A HONKA HONK HONK!"

(trumpet) "TRINK..ATRINK..ATRINKA TRINK TRINK!"

(trumpet) "TRINK..ATRINK..ATRINKA TRINK TRINK!"

(harmonica) "HEMM...DEM...ADEM..ADEM DEM"

(harmonica) "HEMM...DEM...ADEM..ADEM DEM"

Doreathea is in her stoic pose.......hands clasped at her midsection   like most opera singers and then she lets loose in classical tradition:

"*Ave Maria*

Ave Maria

Full of Grace

Gratia plena

Mary, Full of Grace

Maria, gratia plena

Hail, Hail lord

Ave, ave dominus

The Lord is with thee

Dominus tecum

Blessed are you among women

Bendicta tu in melieribus

And blessed

Et benedictus

And blessed is the fruit of your womb

Et benedictus fructus ventris

In your womb, Jesus

Ventris tui, Iesus

Ave Maria

Ave Maria

Mid song..........she shifts everything of her appearance.

"Let's add a little swing to this for my friend Diddley Squatt.... OK!"

She unclasps her hands, and instead starts snapping her fingers and bouncing to the funky beat.....moving funky unlike what she has ever moved before and the group has ever experienced. The band behind her goes wild. THEY HAD NEVER SEEN THIS SIDE OF DORTHEA. The tour's classical Princess actually starts funky dancing! She dances and swings for awhile – and then moves back to the microphone, and without missing a beat – completes the song: in the funky tone:

Ave Maria

Ave Maria

Maiden mild

Maiden mild

I listen to a maid's prayer

I listen to a maiden's prayer

For thou canst hear amid the wild

For thou canst hear amid the wild

'Tis thou, 'tis thou canst save me amid despair

Tis thou, 'tis thou canst save me amid despair

We slumber safely 'til the morrow

We slumber safely 'til the morrow

Though e'en by men outcast reviled

Though e'en by men outcast reviled

Oh, maiden

Oh, maiden

See a maiden sorrow

See a maiden sorrow

Oh, mother hear a suppliant child

Oh, mother hear a suppliant child

Ave Maria

Ave Maria

After the last verse, the crowd stands and gives her a standing ovation. Dorethea is throwing kisses and bowing to the crowd, and after awhile Diddley moves to the center microphone about ready to bring on the next act – but Dorethea rushes and grabs the mic before Diddley reaches it. She says:

"Wait…. I got one last verse to present to you before I exit this stage tonight. Diddley mentioned that the name of this song and music…. i thing you youngsters call it a "groove"…..that's Ok – I'll call it a groove…..but I have to add my two cents to the theme of "You Never Go Against Your Heart", which I think is a great title for a song and life itself; any song or any life. So here are my thoughts about this song theme….and I'm going back to my early country roots with this - just remember – like a lot of us old-timers on this stage tonight – I've never improvised something like this……… but I'm willing to try……here goes my attempt at doing this "rapping" thingy:

"Now Y'all know I never done nothing like you just heard,

But music is just inside you,

And you just have to dig………………………………….and you dig hard

So, don't be surprised about me swaying to a different beat

And saying stuff like Doreathea has never said,

Cause tonight is a different night,

And Dorethea Ain't Never Going against her heart!

Don't be afraid if you are a little different,

Cause we all were born into this great big ball of a world and we had no choice

So, you just have to learn and listen and grow

As your life passes and you experience good and bad stuff,

Cause the good and bad is gonna happen,

And it all and smooth – you gonna get a lot of ruff

You may get a call from the devil

You may get a call from God

But just remember than when the seed is planted

You had no control over

The ground you live – or the type of sod,

So tonight, I'm done with this performance,

And I hope you all had a good time and my shoot was a dart

And I thank young Diddley Squatt

Because I never go and sing against my heart!"

Dorethea then again bows- and the crowd goes wild once again! She then exits to the left of the stage. King D.D., Stan, and all the other performers grab Dorethea and hug her like they've never hugged before. She looks back to the stage – and blows Diddley a final kiss......

Diddley takes center stage again:

"Wow- what a performance.....was that fantastic or what? Dorethea – you were great and I can't thank you enough for participating on this weird, wacky night of music and song. Thank you.

Diddley says, "OK band – kick it back to the faster funky beat." The band immediately obliges- and the beat is back faster.

Diddley:

"Next.... I want to bring to the stage one of the funniest human beings on earth as well as one of my many mentors- like you've seen previously tonight. This man has given me such good advice while I've been on this first tour – and he's helped me understand that humor can help get you through some tough times. So band....... KEEP THE FUNKY GROOVE KNOCKING – and let's welcome to the stage once again the great Slappy Fox!

The band of course continues its funky beat:

(drums) "BA BA BA BOOM"

(organ) "SHACKA LACKA LACKA"

(drums) "BOOM"

(organ) "SHACKA LACKA LACKA"

(drums) "BOOM"

(organ) "SHACKA LACKA LACKA"

(drums) "BOOM"

(organ) "SHACKA LACKA LACKA"

(guitar) "RING DINGA LINGA FINGA

(guitar) "RING DINGA LINGA FINGA

(bass) "RUMP RUMPA RUMPA PUMP"

(bass) "RUMP RUMPA RUMPA PUMP"

(sax) "HONK...A HONK...A HONKA HONK HONK!"

(sax) "HONK...A HONK...A HONKA HONK HONK!"

(trumpet) "TRINK..ATRINK..ATRINKA TRINK TRINK!"

(trumpet) "TRINK..ATRINK..ATRINKA TRINK TRINK!"

(harmonica) "HEMM...DEM...ADEM..ADEM DEM"

(harmonica) "HEMM...DEM...ADEM..ADEM DEM"

Slappy Fox runs on stage squawking and flapping his arms like a bird, running from one side of the stage to the another, while the crowd goes wild laughing and giggling at Slappy's wild entrance....as Slappy continues to flap and make funny faces and dances he almost trips (a couple of times in humor) as he jitterbugs across the stage. He finally lands at center stage and center microphone:

"So let me do my rap, wrap, scrap-

whatever he called it:

"Slappy Fox back at center stage

Maybe to turn a little page

Doing this with love and not rage

I know some of ya'll not of age

And you probably wish I was in a cage!"

The crowd erupts with laughter!

Slappy laughs and stops dancing, and moves dead center:

"Really.... thank you sir Diddley Squatt for closing the show here and in this different way. Wow- I've been on this Chitlin Circuit Tour for many years and I must say I've never seen the headliner, Treach, turn over the closing performance to a newbie and just let him improvise like to tonight…..but I must say I LIKE IT! You know I was just in my dressing room and thinking of some new jokes…..and before it was time for me to come on….I got a couple of "knocks" on my door and I thought of a couple of crazy knock-knock jokes…OK…these are duds…but here goes:

Slappy: "KNOCK KNOCK"

Crowd: "WHO'S THERE?"

Slappy: "BEN HUR"

Crowd: "BEN HUR WHO?"

Slappy: "BEN HUR OVER AND I'll TAKE IT FROM THERE!'

The crowd is in hysterics:

Slappy: "KNOCK KNOCK"

Crowd: "WHO'S THERE?"

Slappy: "TEX"

Crowd: "TEX WHO?"

Slappy: "IT TEXS TWO TO TANGO!'

Slappy: "KNOCK KNOCK"

Crowd: "WHO'S THERE?"

Slappy: "IVANA"

Crowd: "IVANA WHO?"

Slappy: "IVANA HAVE A GOOD TIME- DO YOU?"

Slappy continues:

"Ok.... enough corny knock-knock jokes. However, like everyone else tonight, I just got to add my feelings about this new sing/song Diddley is pushing......this song about "Never Going Against Your Heart" – which I think is true for not only a singer and musicians.... but comedians....and actually all you folks sitting out there tonight. Whatever the hell you are doing to make a living.... picking whatever in somebody's whatever field.... or raising kids.....or hoping to be a comedian or a musician........I must admit that you should never go against your heart.

"And so, what's kind of funny about this subject is that the heart, is without a doubt the most important organ of our body – right? If your heart gives out – call the mortician.... but y'all will probably call your preacher first. But there are simple jokes that need to be said because your heart needs happiness if it is going to keep operating properly – just like everything else......we need funny. So...

"Why did Alfred send pictures of his heart X-ray to his girlfriend every month? Because he wanted to show his "heart" was in the right place!"

"What did the drum say to the drumstick? My heart beats for you."

"Why did the skeleton of Rufus refuse to propose to his girlfriend? I guess his heart wasn't in it?"

"A 92-year-old man named Papa T was asked what was the key to longevity and long life. He said it's easy................ DON'T DIE!"

"Why do so many musicians end up with heart surgery? Because they play their hearts out!"

"Why do gardeners get all the best-looking girls? Because they have the biggest beets!"

"How did the girl know her boyfriend was in love with her? He had a huge "heart" on!"

"Two red blood cells fell in love....... but it was all in "vein."

"What do you call two birds in love? "Tweethearts."

LAUGHTER FROM THE CROWD

"Anyway......I could keep going on all night with heart jokes....but I must move on and let the show proceed. But I just want everyone to know how much I appreciate this young Diddley Squatt to close out his first show – and it just shows how smart this young cat was to get help and let others help him bring it home. So thank you all, and now, before I get a heart attack.............it's time for Slappy to take a nappy" says Slappy as he flaps his wings and starts running around the stage in his famous Slappy Fox exit routine

The crowd goes wild with laughter and applauds as Slappy flaps and eventually exits the stage. Dorethea, Stan, Sam Bluester, Jack Leg Batey – they are of course all there to greet him as he exits the stage to continued laughter and applause. They offer Slappy a towel and he graciously wipes the sweat from his face. Like any other performance, Slappy has given it his all!

Diddley runs to center stage and takes the mic:

"What can you NOT say about Slappy Fox but that he would leave it all on stage. Wow....... you see what I been saying? How lucky am I to have these talented people with me everyday and to learn from them? Thank you Slappy. Now.... let's bring to the stage one of the greatest dancers, not just only on the Chitlin Circuit tour- but I would say one of the greatest, most innovative, dancers in the world today. None other than Jack Leg Batey....and this is going to be very interesting to see how a dancer improvises to a funky new beat. Ladies and gentlemen, welcome to the stage Mr. Jack Leg Batey!"

The funky beat continues:

(drums) "BA BA BA BOOM"

(organ) "SHACKA LACKA LACKA"

(drums) "BOOM"

(organ) "SHACKA LACKA LACKA"

(drums) "BOOM"

(organ) "SHACKA LACKA LACKA"

(drums) "BOOM"

(organ) "SHACKA LACKA LACKA"

(guitar) "RING DINGA LINGA FINGA"

(guitar) "RING DINGA LINGA FINGA"

(bass) "RUMP RUMPA RUMPA PUMP"

(bass) "RUMP RUMPA RUMPA PUMP"

(sax) "HONK...A HONK...A HONKA HONK HONK!"

(sax) "HONK...A HONK...A HONKA HONK HONK!"

(trumpet) "TRINK...ATRINK..ATRINKA TRINK TRINK!"

(trumpet) "TRINK...ATRINK..ATRINKA TRINK TRINK!"

(harmonica) "HEMM...DEM...ADEM..ADEM DEM"

(harmonica) "HEMM...DEM...ADEM..ADEM DEM"

    Jack Leg hops to center stage; one thing different......he has actually taken off his false leg and uses only one leg- something Diddley and the audience had never witnessed before. Jack is holding his false leg in one hand as he dances close around the stage to the funky beat, his tap shoe both in-sync and going against the funky grain of the beat the band has created. What a sight- a man with one leg-twirling and dancing across the stage.

He then stops, and raises his false leg over his head and miraculously spins it on his finger, all while continuing to dance and tap. THE CROWD GOES WILD! Jack then stops again – and plants the leg on the ground and uses it like a cane as he continues his dance......twirling around in circles and circles and circles. He is spinning faster and faster – but along with the funky beat:

"CHONKA CHONKA CHU"

"CHONKA CHONKA CHU"

"CHONKA CHONKA CHU"

He then sits on the floor and re-attaches the leg in a flash; without hesitation, he hops to his feet without using his arms – and is now on both his legs doing his funky dance without missing a beat.

Slappy then runs back on stage and grabs the microphone and starts to talk as his friend continues to dance across the stage with both legs:

Slappy: "It doesn't matter if you lose a hand, arm or a leg arm or a leg

What matters is how you carry on your life- you don't need to beg

        This dude can outdance, out jangle anyone and that's the truth

        The man can outstep Mr. Bojangles; can outhit Babe Ruth!

Peg leg then dances to the microphone and swipes it from Slappy.

Jack Leg: "I'm a dancer, and never been much good at speak

        But if there is one thing I do know

        Is that you have to dig deep if you wanna reach your peak

        My heart is where I start my day

        And for that God is my teacher

        I've been all over this country dancing and tapping

        And its because of my heart- no doggone preacher

        So, I repeat what's been featured on stage tonight,

        and that is "You NEVER Go against your heart"

        And even if you lose at something in life

        Your great heart will never DEPART!"

Jack then twirls around……..does the splits……get's up, grabs Slappy around his shoulders…..and the two do a funky dance off the stage…….dancing……hugging…….dancing.

THE CROWD ONCE AGAIN GOES WILD!

Diddley rushes center stage as the crowd continues with its applause.

"Was that fantastic or what!' Diddley shouts to the enthusiastic sky noise, "It just shows how talented and great these entertainers are………. remember…..NONE of this was perceived before tonight or has ever been practiced or done like this before……..we are just winging it? And, I have to give a big shout out to the city of Atlanta, Georgia! We greatly appreciate your response and understanding to this different ending of our show………you folks have been unbelievable.

So now we have maybe our last performer for tonight……. maybe………maybe not………and there would be nobody better to offer his take on the night than one of the greatest blues singer ever….none other than Sam Bluester. Sam…..please come on out and give us a little something….the man with one of the smoothest voices ever…..and maybe spread some of your thoughts about the heart and what you've learned and seen over all the years you've been in this business. Ladies and gentlemen – the great Sam Bluester."

Sam comes to centerstage and gives Diddley a hug as he is handed the microphone.

'Folks…. I too, like the others have mentioned…….I am not good at improvising or inventing stuff or songs off the top of my head. I'm maybe one of the oldest guys on this tour…. maybe (laughs) - but I want to help Diddley in anyway I can. So……. just let me sing a blues song that I learned a long time ago, and like tonight's theme I will change the lyrics up a bit. It will of course be a little more upbeat because of this funky tune the group has created."

The funky beat continues:

(drums) "BA BA BA BOOM"

(organ) "SHACKA LACKA LACKA"

(drums) "BOOM"

(organ) "SHACKA LACKA LACKA"

(drums) "BOOM"

(organ) "SHACKA LACKA LACKA"

(drums) "BOOM"

(organ) "SHACKA LACKA LACKA"

(guitar) "RING DINGA LINGA FINGA

(guitar) "RING DINGA LINGA FINGA

(bass) "RUMP RUMPA RUMPA PUMP"

(bass) "RUMP RUMPA RUMPA PUMP"

(sax) "HONK...A HONK...A HONKA HONK HONK!"

(sax) "HONK...A HONK...A HONKA HONK HONK!"

(trumpet) "TRINK..ATRINK..ATRINKA TRINK TRINK!"

(trumpet) "TRINK..ATRINK..ATRINKA TRINK TRINK!"

(harmonica) "HEMM...DEM...ADEM..ADEM DEM"

(harmonica) "HEMM...DEM...ADEM..ADEM DEM"

Sam sings:

"I was born by a lake, in a little hut

Oh, and just like that little lake, my life was a rut

My dad wasn't around, and so mom raised us all

But if I fell down, I always stood back up - and stood tall

It's been quite awhile a coming, and I'll never really depart

And I know, I will Never Go Against my Heart

So the years have passed, and I've learned quite a bit

But something I truly learned, is that to never quit

You can be bullied, spat on, and called all kinds of names

But you don't let that deter you – get your ass back in the game!

It's been quite awhile a coming, and I'll never really depart

And I know, I will Never Go Against my Heart

So an easy life is not promised to no one, that's just the way it is

Ups and downs, ins-and-outs, topsy turfy-curfy, the land of Oz and Wiz

It's been a long time a coming, but this I know for sure

You Never Go Against Your Heart, and you will need no special cure

So keep pushing my brothers and sisters, Cause we don't know what's in the sky

If you give everything on earth while living, you will never be afraid when you die!

It's been quite awhile a coming, and I'll never really depart

And I know, I will Never Go Against my Heart"

The music slows and then Sam takes a bow…..forever the gentlemen.

THE CROWD GIVES HIM THUNDEROUS APPLAUSE AS SAM CONTINUES TO BOW AND BLOW KISSES TO THE CROWD. HE THEN EXITS THE STAGE. Diddley takes over center stage:

"Man…….Sam Bluester is truly one of the best bluesmen ever….coming up with that blues song to fit what we are talking about the heart? Now…that's a professional! So we got about who knows how much time left to go until midnight when we have to shut down the show – and we've had all the prior acts come out and improvise on this "You Never Go Against Your Heart" night. So……. I'd say we have at least one more performance to gig with you Atlanta folks before we hid the road to our next stop. We've pretty much exhausted our regular roster, but I'm sure we can" …………BUT BEFORE DIDDLEY CAN FINISH HIS NEXT WORDS – **TESSA TREU** COMES DASHING OUT FROM THE SIDE OF THE STAGE:

"WAIT………. WE NOT DONE YET………I GOT SOMETHING I WANT TO SAY!" Tessa shouts and then grabs the microphone from Diddley.

Tessa is wearing her customary tight short-mini-dress from her earlier performance, and her high heeled shoes. However, Diddley and others immediately notice something a little different about Tessa? Always immaculate with make-up…. her face seems different and off? Diddley looks closer, and he and the audience can detect that Tessa has a huge bruise on her right eye, dropping down to her red cheek. Obviously, Tessa has been hit by someone or been in a fight.

"Tessa- are you alright?" said Diddley.

"I'm actually fine!" said Tessa," and tonight is actually fine - not only a special night for you but is going to be a special night for me. First off – I want to give a big thanks to the other woman on this Chitlin Circuit tour who have always been like a special mother to me, and of course I'm talking about the fabulous Doreathea Doolidge as well as my longtime back-up singers. Doreathea- you have always been a mentor to me and I can't tell you how much I appreciate you always being there for me all these years on the tour and helping me and the few other ladies.......especially me through my difficult experiences with Treach and all the other stuff. You were ALWAYS there for me – and I thank you my sister!" Tessa looks to the side of the stage and throws Doreathea a big kiss. Doreathea, seated on the side of the stage next to Kind D.D., Stan, Slappy, Jack leg, and Sam Bluester – stands and throws a return kiss to Tessa.

Tessa continues as the beat picks up:

"So, I'm about to sing a song that I will make up on the spot – but it definitely fits the theme about "Never Going Against Your Heart." You see, something has been going on my life for some time that ain't right....it ain't been right for a long time!"

(Just then the rest of the Tessa Treu back-up singers run on stage and join their friend Tessa.)

"Well- I've had enough – and it's time for Tessa to speak up. So ya'll listen to what I've got to say. Hit me band (Tessa and the girls move to the beat.)

(drums) "BA BA BA BOOM"

(organ) "SHACKA LACKA LACKA"

(drums) "BOOM"

(organ) "SHACKA LACKA LACKA"

(drums) "BOOM"

(organ) "SHACKA LACKA LACKA"

(drums) "BOOM"

(organ) "SHACKA LACKA LACKA"

(guitar) "RING DINGA LINGA FINGA

(guitar) "RING DINGA LINGA FINGA

(bass) "RUMP RUMPA RUMPA PUMP"

(bass) "RUMP RUMPA RUMPA PUMP"

(sax) "HONK...A HONK...A HONKA HONK HONK!"

(sax) "HONK...A HONK...A HONKA HONK HONK!"

(trumpet) "TRINK..ATRINK..ATRINKA TRINK TRINK!"

(trumpet) "TRINK..ATRINK..ATRINKA TRINK TRINK!"

(harmonica) "HEMM...DEM...ADEM..ADEM DEM"

(harmonica) "HEMM...DEM...ADEM..ADEM DEM"

Tessa sings:

"As everyone has said tonight

You Never Go Against Your Heart

And you've heard all the "whys"

You've heard all the various reasons

But I'm about to tell y'all a little story right now

And I hope you listen to every word I sing and say

Because some people will use your weaknesses and eat them

And you will end up being beaten!

See, some people will tell you things

That they think only you want to hear

But, in actuality, they are only saying these things

To instill in you a special secret fear

They are moving you in a direction

With the only reason to get in your head

But these folks don't give a damn about you

They don't even care if you end up dead!

I have been a singer and dancer

since I first started from scratch

And I fell in love with this man

Thinking he was for me – and we were a perfect match

He was nice at the beginning

and we got married as a couple to succeed

But then I learned all he wanted me for was to help out with his career

And he didn't care about any of my needs

So, we've been touring for years and making some good music

And I guess we've been making some good money

But all these years I've been pushed aside and haven't seen a dime

But I know my Treach has plenty of other honeys

> THE CROWD LET'S OUT A HUGE GASP OF "OH OH" AND CAN TELL THE SONG IS ABOUT TO GET VERY INTERESTING.

Back to Tessa's song:

So just tonight, my "man" hit me in the face once more

Like he's done time and time and time and time again

And all the make-up in the world can't hide the scar

But tonight, I won't hide- cause I know I'm among friends

You should never hit someone you "love"

No matter what the circumstance

And, I know I'm no bird or dove

I'm the one responsible for what I thought was a love dance

So, I'm leaving this man Treach and his band after tonight

and yes, I'm announcing it now

Because I will "Never Go Against My Heart" Again

I'll never have to take another blow against my brow

And I encourage any of you ladies

Who may have experienced similar circumstances as me

Stand up and be yourself as you move forward

Be my roots – and don't fall far from my tree

My name is Tessa Treu,
known as part of the Treach and Tessa Treu Revue

And I want the world to know

That we all have a heart that must be true

So, In closing this song tonight

And please…. please…hear this part

I AM LEAVING TREACH TREU

Because – I'm "Never Going Against My Heart!"

THE CROWD GOES WILD AS TESSA THROWS THE MICROPHONE TO THE GROUND AND EXITS TOWARDS THE STAGE WHERE THE PREVIOUS PERFORMERS WERE SITTING BUT NOW ALL STAND AND APPLAUD.

However………before Tessa can exit the stage and get to her friends, TREACH TREU BURST THRU the same side and no one can hold him back….TREACH IS LIVID!

"IMA GET YOU BITCH – NO ONE EMBARASSES TREACH TREU IN PUBLIC THE WAY YOU JUST DID- I MADE YOU WHO YOU ARE!!" Before all the fellas can stop Treach – **he bust through their arms and full fist hits Tessa in her other eye- and blood splatters over the stage as she falls to the ground.**

THE CROWD GASPS IN DISBELIEF!

Sam, Jack-Leg, King D.D., and Diddley – all the fellas are eventually able to grab Treach, and soon the facilities security personnel tackle Treach and bring him to the ground. Tessa steps around the melee on the ground and runs around them and heads to centerstage:

"You are all witnesses tonight – this man assaulted me in full view of you all. I'm sure one day in the future they will have cameras in all these venues to capture what goes on……maybe one day in the future they will invent phones with cameras or something like that – but at least now everyone knows what I have been going through and it ends tonight. So…..I may be bloodied…..but I am blessed that everyone was here to witness what goes on to far too many women performers lives. But for me – THIS ENDS TONIGHT!

As the security forces secure Treach (thou he continues to yell and scream) – he finally stands up, and with his hands tied behind his back, is lead away out the back to who knows whatever may happen.

"YOU BITCH!" he screams for the last time as he is led away.

Diddley moves to center stage and addresses the crowd:

"Well……WOW…..I guess this is one of the most interesting and different closing performances we have all ever witnessed. But I must say in the end…..I'm pretty happy. I think the whole world knew what Tessa was going through….and now hopefully she can't be harmed anymore and go on with her dreams of singing and dancing, and producing joy to the world in peace. What a night……….I guess this ends it……we only have a ½ hour left before the law states we have to close down….so…….."

But just then the performers from the side of the stage all come running to center stage and stops Diddley's exit speech. Dorethea takes the microphone.

"Young Diddley……, since we do have a little time left – we have **TWO** last performers who want to contribute to this weird night. This first person is a young man you met recently and he came and told us all about a conversation you had with him….and it helped give him hope for the future of America………and that he just wants to thank you by the only means he knows how. Now…. I…and the rest of the Chitlin Circuit Tour, have played with various musicians of all colors…we've never cared……but tonight we hope is a special night for you and we hope this is a learning experience. So please……….in the little time left……..just jam with your "two" new found friends, and we think it will benefit you both and be a fitting end to the "You Never Go Against Your Heart" theme of tonight's very unique show – and when I say unique – I've been around 40 years and never seen a night like tonight. So here is our FIRST special guest to close out the show with you," as the Chitlin

Tour performers exit the stage:

OUT FROM THE STAGE COMES WHITE BOY RIGHTEOUS CLEMENS – WITH AN ELECTRIC BASS STRAPPED AROUND HIS NECK. He moves to the microphone:

"I hope you folks don't mind. But I just met this amazing young man… and I just have to play with him before I jump back on the road and play with my other band. See……..I've never said this before- but I LOVE black musicians. We discussed meeting up in the future……..but you never know when the future is…right? So, I thought before I left – I'd make the future tonight. Mr. Diddley Squatt – grab your guitar – and let's close out this incredible "funky" night because like you told me earlier – "YOU NEVER GO AGAINST YOUR HEART!"

DIDDLEY RUNS OVER AND GRABS RIGHTEOUS AROUND THE NECK AND THEY HUG AND SMILE. Diddley grabs his guitar around his neck – and of course the band kicks in with its funky beat!

(drums) "BA BA BA BOOM"

(organ) "SHACKA LACKA LACKA"

(drums) "BOOM"

(organ) "SHACKA LACKA LACKA"

(drums) "BOOM"

(organ) "SHACKA LACKA LACKA"

(drums) "BOOM"

(organ) "SHACKA LACKA LACKA"

(guitar) "RING DINGA LINGA FINGA"

(guitar) "RING DINGA LINGA FINGA"

(sax) "HONK...A HONK...A HONKA HONK HONK!"

(sax) "HONK...A HONK...A HONKA HONK HONK!"

(trumpet) "TRINK..ATRINK..ATRINKA TRINK TRINK!"

(trumpet) "TRINK..ATRINK..ATRINKA TRINK TRINK!"

(harmonica) "HEMM...DEM...ADEM..ADEM DEM"

(harmonica) "HEMM...DEM...ADEM..ADEM DEM"

Diddley starts off with a simple guitar rift – just in tune with the basic beat.

Righteous jumps in in tune – with a funky bass beat complementing Diddley's rift.

Righteous on bass:

(bass) "RUMP RUMPA RUMPA PUMP"

(bass) "RUMP RUMPA RUMPA PUMP"

Diddley changes chords – moving up and down – challenging Righteous

Righteous changes cords – accepting the challenge - right in tune with Diddley – and they both laugh.

(bass) "RUMPING RUMPING RUMPING PUMPING"

(bass) "RUMPING RUMPING RUMPING PUMPING"

Diddley drops a chord – and slides to the left

Righteous drops to the same chord- and slides to the right

THEY BOTH LAUGH AT EACH OTHER …..however not missing a funky guitar and bass lick……I MEAN THEY ARE JAMMING!

Dorethea then runs on stage and grabs the microphone – nobody stops playing- and Dorethea says:

"HOLD ON……..Mr. Diddley Squatt – we have ONE LAST guest performer to introduce to the world tonight.

And WHO comes from the right of the stage? NONE OTHER THAN **MUTE** WITH A GUITAR STRUNG AROUND HIS NECK.

"Now folks…. this young man is called Mute. He has been helping out on various Chitlin Tours for many years……. setting up and taking down our instruments and packing them up from city to city. The thing is – Mute can't talk in a regular way. He can hear….and he can mouth certain words – but believe me he don't talk like most of us…..that's how he got the name Mute. But one thing – we all respect Mute because he is such a hard worker. And although we've seen him tinkering around with just about every instrument you see on stage – none of us really knew he could actually play an instrument. However, since tonight is such a different and special night invented by Mr. Diddley Squatt- everything is on the table!"

THE CROWD ERUPTS INTO APPLAUSE AND LAUGHTER.

"So…..hold onto your hats ladies and gentlemen………for Mute, our longtime roadie, will step on this stage as a first time performer……..Mute has joined the band for tonight," said Dorethea.

Mute hits center stage and lets out a funky guitar lick that sounds like it itself is speaking….it squeaks:

"HEEEEEEEEEEEEEEEEAHHHHHHHHHHH HEAAAAAAAAAAAAAH;"""""

"HEEEEELLLLLLLLOOOOOOOOOOOOO EVEEEERRRYYYBOOOODY"

(drums) "BA BA BA BOOM"

(organ) "SHACKA LACKA LACKA"

(drums) "BOOM"

(organ) "SHACKA LACKA LACKA"

(drums) "BOOM"

(organ) "SHACKA LACKA LACKA"

(drums) "BOOM"

(organ) "SHACKA LACKA LACKA"

(guitar) "RING DINGA LINGA FINGA

(guitar) "RING DINGA LINGA FINGA

bass) "RUMPING RUMPING RUMPING PUMPING"

(bass) "RUMPING RUMPING RUMPING PUMPING"

(sax) "HONK...A HONK...A HONKA HONK HONK!"

(sax) "HONK...A HONK...A HONKA HONK HONK!"

(trumpet) "TRINK..ATRINK..ATRINKA TRINK TRINK!"

(trumpet) "TRINK..ATRINK..ATRINKA TRINK TRINK!"

(harmonica) "HEMM...DEM...ADEM..ADEM DEM"

(harmonica) "HEMM...DEM...ADEM...ADEM DEM"

The crowd rises in applause.

Mute moves back.

Righteous moves to the microphone:

"Music is for all people – doesn't matter your race, creed, or color

Diddley runs to the microphone:

"Righteous is correct – music is all about making us all love fuller

Righteous:

"So, You Never Go Against Your Heart – let's all take a stand in unison tonight

Diddley:

"As you saw with Tessa tonight – you can't win if you don't put up a fight

Righteous:

"This has been quite an experience - and I'm glad it all wasn't too intense

Diddley:

"I'm glad we were able to combine Diddley, Righteous, and Mute "who me?"-this was indeed a "Who Me" Hendrix Experience!

THE CROWD STANDS AND THERE IS DANCING IN THE AISLES AS DIDDLEY, RIGHTEOUS, AND MUTE JUST PLAY CRAZY MUSIC TO THE FUNKY BEAT……EVEN THE SECURITY GUARDS ARE DANCING AND JUMPING UP ON CHAIRS. ALL THE PREVIOUS PERFORMERS RUN ON STAGE AND DANCE AS DIDDLEY, RIGHEOUS, AND MUTE TEAR IT UP! Finally…. the music is winding down. All the performers and others representing the Chitlin Circuit Tour stand in line and join arms:

Pee Wee, King D.D., Stan the Lizard Man, Dorethea Doolidge, Slappy Fox, Jack Leg Batey, Sam Bluester, Tessa Treu and her Revue, Righteous Clemens, Diddley Squatt, Mute, the entire Chitlin Tour Band – THEY ALL TAKE A BOW.

Diddley to the microphone:

"GOODNIGHT ATLANTA – THANK YOU FOR A NIGHT THAT I AND THE CHITLIN CIRCUIT PERFORMERS WILL NEVER FORGET! SPREAD JOY IN THE WORLD……BE KIND TO EVERYONE…. LIVE YOUR BEST LIFE…..AND JUST REMEMBER TO :

"NEVER GO AGAINST YOUR HEART"

The performers take a final bow:

The APPLAUSE CONTINUES.......

And finally......the curtain closes while the crowd is still yelling but exiting......

Finally.... OVER!

DONE....

OVER....

WHEW!!!!!!!!!!!!!!!!!!!!!!!!!!!!!!

OVER.......

OVER!!!!!!!!!!!!!!!!!!!

done...............

Chapter 9
If You Don't Know Diddley – You Don't Know Squatt

Diddley back in his room....exhausted after such an amazing and exquisite night. He layed on the bed and folded his arms around his stomach, staring at the ceiling. While Diddley's body is tired and he is sure he needs a good night's sleep before they head to the next leg of the tour in the morning – some city in Florida- Diddley is just *too* pumped-up to what just ended......Diddley closing his first show, and in such a strange manner of just winging it and improvising and going with the flow of whatever happens.......and others agree with your crazy idea ....and it all HAPPENED!

"That was some CRAZAY music out there tonight!" said Sly as he jumped on the bed- board over Diddley's head. Sly leaned down and Diddley sees him from upside down – Sly making squirrel faces with his big eyes and huge squirrel teeth – ending with a huge squirrel grin on his face.

"I just love that you decided to improvise the closing number. When has that ever been done before on the Chitlin Circuit? I can tell you not since we've been on board.... nobody has had the gall or the balls to try such a stunt", said Sly as he scrambled from one side of the headboard to the other he was so excited.

"Thanks my good friend.....but like the song said.....I just decided to not go against my heart and let everybody try something different. As you know better than anybody else......I like different and new. So now we are gonna have to see the consequences that may happen because of my experiment. I think all my performer friends were excited – but Treach Treu has got to be pissed at me – and who knows if he will be arrested or jailed or what may happen.....and then what happens to Tessa and the rest of the Revue? Have I maybe destroyed careers?."

Suddenly a knock at the door?

"Oh oh.... somebody is at the door...... I better hide," said Sly as he grabs a nut he left on the headboard and runs into the tiny closet.

Diddley moved to the door and opened it, and is surprised to find all the members of the Treach Treu Revue (except Treach) at the door, including Tessa and her backing singers........they are all half-dressed, part clothes-part pajamas; some with shoes and socks, others barefooted and open collars...... and some have champaign bottles in their hands.

"LET US IN DIDDLEY – WE GOT TO TELL YOU THANK YOU!" they shout in happiness and spray champagne as they enter throughout the room. Tessa and the girls barge into the room with the group.

"We are free!" they all shout. The guitar player explains: "No more Treach beating up on Tessa and we can't talk about it........let that Treach get himself a new band who doesn't have to watch his relentless beating of Tessa and tell us we better not spill the beans.......WE ARE ALL FREE AFTER TONIGHT AND IT IS BECAUSE OF DIDDLEY SQUATT!"'

Tessa moves to Diddley and stands directly in front of him. Tears fill her eyes. The room goes silent as Tessa speaks.

"Young Diddley Squatt – we are all here for a quick thank you for what you did tonight. Not just closing the show and spoiling Treach's attempt at having you fail at your first closing – it was his idea at having you close the show – in hopes that you would fail and get kicked off the Chitlin Circuit Tour. He was trying to ruin your young and burgeoning career....for various reasons

" But I still don't know exactly why?" asked Diddley.

"I'll tell you why, young Diddley" said Tessa while looking

deeply into Diddley's eyes..........." because Treach doesn't give a flying FUCK about anybody but himself! He doesn't care about me....his wife.........his band...all he cares about is Treach Treu and the band trying to make money – most of the money of which he keeps by the way. HE CARES ABOUT HIM ONLY! The guy is a trump funk!"

"My" says Diddley looking into Tessa's eyes with truthfulness........." I like that term a Trump Funk....I'll definitely write it in my journal. Sigh.... I just don't understand what I did to him for him wanting me to fail? I never said a bad word to him? I loved your performances and all that the Revue put on? I love all the groups and everyone has helped me so much."

"That's what I'm trying to tell you Diddley. This world is not made up with all good-hearted people like you – there are some snakes in this world and all they think about is themselves......even more so in this crazy music business? HA! It is crazier than anything else. So.........I'm saying all this in hopes this is a learning lesson and experience for you – please remember what happened tonight and all those who came to your support. Not everybody is crazy and back-sided – most in this business are here because they love entertaining folks and they love music and trying to bring music as a break and enlightenment for all that every human goes through on a daily basis. The same is with most people in this world – regardless of skin color. Most people are good and just trying to live a good life as you saw and heard after meeting all those folks who came to talk to you from the fields. We entertainers are blessed and lucky to make a living doing what we want to do. So please LEARN from tonight's experience – do not let it bother you from this minute forward – and as you say in many of your songs – GO WITH YOUR HEART! You are a special young man!"

Tessa then grabs Diddley and gives him the tightest hug. Diddley whispers "thank you" into Tessa's ear. All the other members of the Revue in the room run and soon there is an entire group hug........ musicians saying to each other "I LOVE YOU " TO EACH OTHER AND TEARS FLOWING EVERYWHERE."

"OK – LET'S PARTY IN MY ROOM! DIDDLEY – YOU COMING TO THE PARTY?" shouts the saxophone player and everybody rips:

"PARTY!!!!!"

Diddley says "I don't know……………. I'll think about it, but I'm totally exhausted."

"Okay, think about it," they all say.

Everybody gives Diddley a private hug as they exit the room one-by-one, excited about the joyous party that is about to explode.

Tessa is the last one to leave and tells Diddley "You are ONE exceptional young man Diddley Squatt. You are going to go far in this business. Keep writing songs and playing what you feel from your heart – and continue to make us all proud. See you at the next gig……..and words can't describe my feelings for what happened tonight…..for I am free!"

Diddley hits the bed and can't move.

The next morning. Diddley is awoken by Sly who jumps onto the pillow next to him.

"Diddley! WAKE UP WAKE up" says Sly as he is flying across the room.

"I was just downstairs searching for a nut outside this room and I heard the guy at the front desk saying that the big news of the day in this crazy small city was that Tessa Treu is filing for divorce from Treach Treu and the press is going wild.

"That's GREAT news Sly" says Diddley as he playfully

covers the pillow over Sly's small face………….. "why do I always get the best news in the world from my best friend."

The two tumble around the bed…..Sly avoiding Diddley's pillows throws. Finally, Sly settles down and moves to the bedpost directly in front of Diddley.

"Sooooooooooooooooooooooo what's next on the agenda?" says Sly as he grabs a nut and starts chomping.

"Well" says Diddley, "I just happened to overhear some of the performers talking before they left last night….and while our next stop is supposed to be in Florida……..but a hurricane warning has been issued across those areas of the South….and that we may be headed back home to Mississippi to wait and see what happens. Can you believe it? I was just getting comfortable after three performances on my first tour, but we may have to head back home because of a hurricane.

"OH NO!" says Sly, " I too was excited that we would see other parts of this USA and maybe I could meet some other squirrel friends or relatives from the South? Diddley……I was looking forward to more experiences!" said Sly as he scampered around the room in the most distressed manner that Diddley had ever seen his friend.

Diddley turned to Sly, and in a very calm voice, moved closely to him and said "Sly…………….my best friend in the world……..if there is ONE thing I've learned on this tour – it is to expect the unexpected. I too was ready to move on to Georgia and Florida……to meet new folks……and to try out new songs and perform before new audiences. However – we can't predict what may happen in life? Nobody knows what the new day will bring? You wake up in the morning and have an agenda- but only GOD makes the decision on whether that day will happen the way you may want it to go and your agenda will change? God has to make earthly decisions……….. he has a tremendous job every day of the year."

Sly jumps on Diddley's shoulder.

"You are so right my best friend. We can try and project our steps forward – but we cannot control the thing called FATE. So, what if we head back home to Mississippi? Hopefully in a short time we can pick up and visit these next beautiful states and you can put on your shows for them – which will blow their minds."

Diddley and Sly slap high fives.

There is then another knock at the door. Sly scampers to the shelf in the closet again – where he is always able to peer throughout the room without anybody knowing he is even in the room or watching.

Diddley opens the door and there stands W.C. Valley with this weird, stoned look on his face? His face is completely pale and his eyes are wildly opened wide and he looks weird in the eyes - and these eyes look sadly directly into Diddley's eyes. Diddley had never seen the boisterous, usually smiling or smirking – laughing- W.C. in such a somber condition before. No cigar? Finally, gathering his voice to speak, W.C. says to Diddley through stuttered sentences:

"Young……….. young….Diddley….I III II don't don't know if you you heard heard heard……but……… (W.C composes himself)……sigh……… we may have to cancel the rest of the tour and head back to Mississippi immediately. J.J. Abrahms contacted me early this morning and informed me that there is a major hurricane tearing towards down south, especially to the Florida panhandle area that we were heading to on our next Chitlin Tour stop, and that we have been advised that it isn't safe to proceed. I know you had a fantastic night last night – but ain't a damn thing you can do if mother nature calls…….and it appears mom nature will be yelling and screaming in the coming days. Hey….you said you like to write songs from stuff you hear people say….well…..I'm telling you "You Can't Stop Mother Nature When She's About to Feature a Hurricane Creature." – Now…. make that into a song, but just remember that ol W.C. gave you the title and I want my cut if it becomes a hit," W.C. laughs and even Diddley laughs.....W.C. has returned to his old self.

"I understand fully," said Diddley, " we used to have hurricane warnings in Mississippi and Momma-Squatt took in folks at the Copp-A-Squatt just to help out. She and the girls told me there wasn't much you could do but to be safe.....so I understand completely W.C."

"Thanks for understanding young man," said W.C., "So pack up your bags......and later head downstairs to the lobby........ we are about to have a meeting in about an hour with all the performers and staff. Hopefully I'll have more details and we can talk about this."

"No problem," said Diddley, but before he could close the door W.C. catches it with his foot and says:

"But once again youngblood – I just want you to know........I just couldn't stop watching you closing show last night. I've been doing this a long time- and seen more shows than you can imagine – but your closing set was dynamite. Also.....I had secretly heard that Treach was trying to sabotage you and hope you bombed last night – that dirty son-of-a-gun! I'm so glad he got his comeuppance last night. You put on a show for the ages and that dude got dragged to jail at the end- the night couldn't have ended any better. So.........just wanted to say I'm PROUD of you young man.... you are indeed something special."

Diddley and W.C. shook hands.

"You gotta get ready to go to this meeting!" says Sly after W.C. leaves.

The hotel lobby. An hour later.

Meeting

All the performers are in the lobby anxiously awaiting to see exactly what is going on and why W.C. called the meeting – that is, all the performers except Treach Treu- who everyone assumes he is still behind bars someplace for assaulting Tessa in front of the entire crowd last night. W.C. steps to the front of the room and begins talking:

"To all my wonderful Chitlin Circuit Tour Performers - I have some important news to share by way of the President of the Chitlin Tour, Mr. J. J. Abrahms. Number one, the remaining tour dates and concert shows that were to be included in this edition of the Chitlin Circuit Tour have unfortunately been cancelled due to sever hurricane warnings expected to hit in the cities we were headed – mainly in the state of Florida. Therefore, it is within the best interest of management that the tour be halted and we return to Mississippi – MAINLY FOR THE SAFETY of all our performers, acts, and stage crew. Your safety is our ultimate concern. In short- no way in HELL do we want to be caught up in that mess!"

The performers laugh at W.C.'s honesty.

"If things change after we return, we can hop back on the Betty B and head back down to Florida for rescheduled shows- but we heading home for now folks. So, if you haven't started packing – best be getting started so we can head out sometimes this afternoon – we want to beat this thing before it beats us! "

Now....... I just got some other news that is both good and bad – and is definitely a reason for us to head back home. This one is gonna be hard to say....... because I just had a heartfelt talk with the young man most affected by what the news I'm about to express........and that news is..........is.............SHIT THIS IS HARD......."

W.C looks dead into Diddley's eyes and says:

"J.J. Abrahms just informed me that this one involves our beloved Momma Squatt – the owner of the Copp-A-Squatt Inn and your grandma."

Diddley shoots up out of his seat!

"OH NO – WHAT HAPPENED" Diddley shouts as gasps fill the lobby.

"I'm sorry Diddley – I know we just talked – but I just got the telegraph from J.J.………our beloved Momma Squatt, your grandmother, has taken ill and was recently rushed to the hospital in Rundown City. That's all I know……. but the note said she made it to the hospital and is in good hands, and hopefully will be OK. All our prayers are with your beloved grandma!"

All the performers run over to Diddley and help comfort him as he still stands in shock…. soon come the words of encouragement and love:

"Be strong young buck – she will be OK."

"Our prayers are with you Diddley."

"Momma Squatt is a fighter young man – she will pull through!"

"Prayers up in heaven young Diddley – God is watching over her."

"Thank you all for your kind words" says Diddley as he finds a seat.

"You are all right – my grandmother is a fighter and a strong woman! If there was ever one person who would exemplify our song about "You Never Go Against Your Heart "– I think we can agree it would be Momma Squatt.

W.C. finishes his talk:

"I know this has been devasting news to us all – but it is kinda a good thing overall if you think about it? Yeah.... bad that we can't finish the tour.......but good that we are heading home and will be able to check on Momma Squatt. So.... I dunno.... sometimes they say things happen for a reason, O.K.........I'm done. Let's go pack and meet everyone at the Betty Boop in a couple of hours. We all just gotta go with the flow!"

As they exit the room, W.C pulls Diddley aside and whispers:

"If you remember, when you signed your contract it said all the performers would be paid at the end of the tour. Well....... we know the tour will be interrupted and everyone needs some money in-between. So- you and the others will be receiving a stipend from your tour check once we get home and off the bus in Rundown, Mississippi. J.J. is going to throw in a little extra in case you need it to help out with Momma Squatt, who J.J. also loved. Don't tell the others about this - I will tell them when we get home....... but I wanted to tell you first. Now – if you ain't ever had a bank account, let me know and I can help you arrange it back home. Be smart with your money."

"Thank you, Mr. W.C.... this will be the first time I've ever been paid for something like this. Thank you, sir!" said Diddley.

Diddley back in his room. He had already cried his tears and is resolved to the fact that Momma Squatt is ill – but he is happy that he will be heading back and hopefully get back to help out in any way he can or is needed. Diddley is packed and ready.

Before they leave, Diddley moseys over and pulls the curtains. He looks out into a great open field that stretches for long periods....... looking out into the world that has always calmed him.... fields on one side filled with green pastures, trees, corn and other vegetable products – and then to the left – jacketed construction crews working on a new "freeway" and Diddley can see some buildings to the left. So.... there is nature – but there is also nurture (society) growing. Diddley pauses.......and it hits him.... this is what the future will look like. A little of the old....and a little of the new – and surely in time – the new will overtake the old.

Sly runs up and hops on Diddley's shoulder.

"Surely, you know how much I love Momma Squatt- no words needed. But as we've discussed since this tour began, there comes a time to move on......and now is the time to move on.......... time to hit the bus youngblood," says Sly while looking out the window – a last time for both of them.

Diddley has his guitar bag, his clothes bags – everything slung over his shoulder.

"Yes....it is time to move on to our next adventure," says Diddley," and let's just remember that life is unpredictable. But, I predict, we will have good days in the future. I'm just blessed that my best friend has been here to experience all this with me. We got to get back and help Momma Squatt and the girls anyway we can – and that is the best part. Some folks may think it is tragic to end the tour early – but this coming hurricane may be prophetic."

Sly slides into his guitar pouch.

Diddley closes the door as they step outside and they head down the stairs toward the Betty B.

"Prophetic? What does that mean? Never heard you use that word before?" said Sly from his hidden pouch.

Diddley speaks:

"It just means that men, women, humans- they don't control the world or what happens. Only God controls the world-

and he does it in his own and sneaky way. Diddley Squatt being on his first tour....... meeting and getting to know all the men and women performers on this tour....the Treach and Tessa Treu situation....... My first fights.... meeting Mute and Righteous Clemons.........talking to all the brothers working in the various fields during our Betty Boop rides....... Playing "Moments That Take Your Breath Away" and "You Never Go Against Your Heart" ....and now having to cut short the tour and heading back home because of nature and nurture - the hurricane- Momma Squatt...........it's all just God's prophecy leading us and I see that clearly. Enough said...So.... let's head to the bus, my best friend."

"That was a great speech," said Sly as he spits out his words from his hidden pouch and they march down the hall.

"So....... I only have one last thing to say."

"What's that?" says Diddley with a quizzical look on his face.

Sly shouts:

"DID YOU REMEMBER TO GET ME SOME NUTS FOR THE LONG TRAIN RIDE HOME?!"

Diddley slowly reaches into his coat pocket............... gently pulls out some nuts.......................and says:

"IF YOU DON'T KNOW DIDDLEY – YOU DON'T KNOW SQUATT!"

The end